*"Who are we but the stories we tell ourselves,
about ourselves, and believe?"*

SCOTT TUROW, *ORDINARY HEROES*

Never give up, Dear Reader.
Together, we can change the world.
                              MC Nelson

CHRYSALIS

a novel

M.C. Nelson

Ideas into Books® WESTVIEW
KINGSTON SPRINGS, TENNESSEE

Chrysalis

ISBN 978-1-62880-781-3 Perfect Bound
ISBN 978-1-62880-077-7 Case Laminate
ISBN 978-1-62880-102-6 Smashwords
ISBN 978-1-62880-060-9 Amazon Kindle
ISBN 978-1-62880-770-7 Audiobook

This is a work of fiction. The names, characters, places, and events described herein are either fictitious or are used in a fictitious manner. Any similarity to actual people, living or dead, places, institutions, or events is purely coincidental.

Third Edition, September 2021.

The cover photograph by Benjamin Spiegel is gratefully used with the permission of Kathleen Nelson Spiegel.

Dr. Susan Ford Wiltshire's translation of Virgil's magnificent words is used with her permission and the author's gratitude.

Special thanks to Scott Turow for permission to use the quotation on the frontispiece from *Ordinary Heroes,* Farrar, Straus and Giroux, New York, 2005, and to *The Paris Review* for permission to use the quote from Chinua Achebe.

Digitally printed on acid-free paper.

Ideas into Books ® WESTVIEW
P.O. Box 605
Kingston Springs, Tennessee 37082
www.ideasintobooks.net

For those who survived,

In memory of those who did not, and

With gratitude for all those who help bring dark secrets to light.

If you've ever found yourself feeling powerless and violated by those you should have been able to trust; while

   trying desperately to be faithful and good;

   taking responsibility for things beyond your control;

   being forced into the position of unwillingly participating in the devastation of someone you wanted to protect;

   believing yourself to be totally abandoned and alone;

   searching for forgiveness and redemption;

   and experiencing at the last, even if not in full, at least the beginnings of Grace where and from whom you did not expect it,

   then you, too, may be a survivor.

Note to Survivors and Those with Tender Hearts:

Please be forewarned that several parts of this book contain graphic descriptions of violence against children and adults.

At the suggestion of several readers, one-sentence synopses of these passages have been provided as an alternative for those who feel profoundly their own pain or the anguish of others. Each of these passages is bulleted next to the section number like this:

❖❖ 0.00 PLACE, DATE ❖❖

If you would like to skip these passages, you will find their synopses on pages 265 and 266.

The sections most likely to trigger trauma in survivors have been further delineated by shading covering the entire page and the mark of this symbol (❖) in the center. A one-sentence synopsis for each one can be found on page 267.

Please take seriously the suggestion to use these synopses. If you're not sure, you might want to ask someone who knows you well to read them and let you know what they think.

Your going on to the next unmarked section won't hurt my feelings at all; indeed, your taking steps to protect yourselves would please me greatly. I do not wish to add to your pain.

If you were one of the children to whom these sorts of things happened, **it wasn't your fault**.

The Author

Sunt hic etiam sua praemia laudi;
sunt lacrimae rerum et mentem mortalia tangunt.
solve metus;
feret haec aliquam tibi fama salutem.

VIRGIL, *AENEID* I.461-463

Even here there are its own rewards for worth;
Even here there are tears in things and
mortal matters touch the heart.
Put away your fear;
this story will bring you some reprieve.

TRANSLATION OF VIRGIL'S *AENEID* I.461-463 BY DR. SUSAN FORD WILTSHIRE

CHAPTER ONE

THE FAMILY

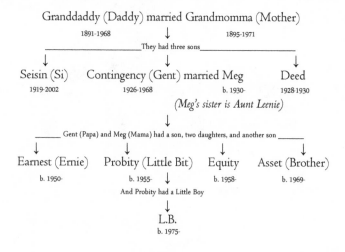

Granddaddy (Daddy) married Grandmomma (Mother)
1891-1968   1895-1971

_____They had three sons_____

| Seisin (Si) | Contingency (Gent) married Meg | | Deed |
| 1919-2002 | 1926-1968 | b. 1930- | 1928-1930 |

(Meg's sister is Aunt Leenie)

_____ Gent (Papa) and Meg (Mama) had a son, two daughters, and another son _____

| Earnest (Ernie) | Probity (Little Bit) | Equity | Asset (Brother) |
| b. 1950- | b. 1955- | b. 1958- | b. 1969- |

And Probity had a Little Boy

L.B.
b. 1975-

1.1 Nashville, Tennessee, 2014

Probity

All of my perpetrators are dead.

I didn't kill them, in case you're wondering. I'm just telling you that on the front end because I'd be wondering about it, myself, if someone said that to me. I didn't get to enjoy any type of closure or revenge— like personally choking the life out of them, or centering them in the crosshairs and experiencing the pull of the trigger, or plunging a knife in them as far as I could get it to go—maybe even more than once, if I could—or anything equally satisfying, even though many times I would've liked to. Some days, I still would. Their being dead is important to the story because it makes the telling of it possible. If they'd lived, I'm sure I'd be the one in the grave by now instead.

And you probably ought to know, too, that most everybody in my family thinks I'm completely out of my cotton-pickin' mind. The only people I know who believe me about what went on back then are shrinks and strangers and folks I've met in the years since from out of town and such, but nobody in my family or in Bumblebee does—at least not anybody who's ever admitted it to me. My grandmomma and granddaddy might've believed me, if they hadn't died. Even my mama, God bless her, says she can't figure out why I keep on lying to her about this when I never lied to her about anything else she ever knew of, not in my whole life.

The part I can't figure out is why it is that if I never lied to her about anything else, what makes her think I'm lying now.

I wouldn't lie about something like this. If someone was going to make up a story, they'd tell someone how brave they are, or how smart, or what they did good, or how they've got lots of money or a big house, or something like that. You wouldn't tell them you were hurt or scared or powerless to protect yourself or someone else. If you were going to make something up, you'd make it make sense. And this never has.

I've got a doctor now who's heard pretty much the whole drawn-out story, and one really good friend who has, too, and a couple more who've heard little-bitty parts of it or teeny-tiny short versions of the whole damn thing. Short like you could tell it in less than an hour, a story that took me my whole life to live. Somehow or another I've stayed out of jail or the hospital or the psych ward the whole time, even on days and nights when I thought there was no way I'd still be alive tomorrow, because the only place they were still alive was inside of my head, and if I had to kill myself to kill them... well, that'd be okay, too.

1.2 BUMBLEBEE, 1968; REMEMBERING 1930

GENT

I've always been fascinated by death, ever since I was a boy. And though I am sure I had seen or known about things dead or dying before then, my first conscious awareness of the termination of life came just over four years after the beginning of my own, with the 1930 death of my younger brother.

The concept of mortality encompasses a plethora of intriguing questions, such as how life comes into being, why it ends and what that means, or why we think about the things we think about when we've realized that there's no question we are dying. Like me, right now. I know that there's not a damn thing anyone else can do to change what's about to happen. No one can save me. No one can change any of the decisions I made that brought me to this place, this moment. It's too late for that now. I know now I don't have much time left. I'm past thinking I am dying generically, someday, like we're all going to go sometime. At this point I'm resigned to the fact that for me, death is coming soon. Quite soon. It's in progress. Now. Fascinating.

And all I can see is that hallway where we were that day when Si and Deed and I were kids, the one outside the apartment we lived in then, upstairs from Daddy's first law office. The one where we were roughhousing, horsing around playing tag when Mother left to go pick up something for supper, and told Si and me to watch Deed until she got home.

"Seisin Hunter Jones, you and Contingency are in charge of Deed till I get back. You watch him, now, 'cause he's just a baby. And stop that horsing around *right now* and behave yourselves till I get home."

Oh, God, I wish we had. But we were boys, just *boys* really, and we *didn't* stop horsing around. Deed was whining because he wanted to watch for Mother out the window, which was open except for the screen, of course, because the day was hot and no one we knew had air conditioning back then. And then one of us picked him up to sit him on the windowsill so he could see, and the other one hit him in the back of the head, just smacked him *one time* because he was driving us crazy with all of his whining and deserved it, and we both agreed that neither one of us would ever tell, not till our dying day, which one of us did which, and we never did. And we didn't mean for him to, we never meant to really hurt him, but he fell right through that screen, fell, fell all the way down the seven stories to the sidewalk below, where Mother was looking up yelling at us to pay attention and stop fooling around and get him out of the window. And we swore later he climbed up there all by himself and we couldn't get to him in time, but we knew what happened.

Si and I never forgot. We always remembered. We always knew.

1.3 BUMBLEBEE, 1931

GRANDDADDY

After Deed died, things were just never the same again. I love my boys' mother more than I do my own life, and losing the baby just plum broke her heart. Mine, too, I reckon.

Deed had been such a sweet, happy boy, and Mother always believed it was her fault for leaving Si— who was eleven by then and tall as a man, but still just a boy himself—in charge of him instead of taking him with her when she ran out just for a minute to pick up what we needed for dinner that night. I thought it was my fault for never making enough money that we could ever buy more than one or two days' worth of food at a time, so Mother could live an easier life than the one she lived before we got married, but we just loved each other so, and we couldn't wait to be together. No one ever knows what direction a life might take. It can turn on a dime.

After Deed, well, neither one of us could bear going home, day after day, up those long stairs into the hallway where he'd been when he fell. It seemed like every day our steps, which used to be so light and eager to get home to the boys and to each other, dragged slower and heavier, until each of us just got to where we dreaded going home at all.

From the law office, just five floors down from the apartment, I could look out the window and down to where he landed. I could see where Mother had been when she saw him, looking up towards home while he fell there across the street right before her eyes. I can still see him falling, see the grocery bag where she dropped it, her running trying to get there in time to catch him, the sidewalk rushing up to meet him, all of it in slow motion in my head, even though I wasn't looking out the window at the time and my eyes didn't see it at all. It may have been fresher and more painful then, but it's never stopped haunting me to this day. He'd been hardly more than a baby, and hadn't even celebrated his second birthday before he died.

I'd been so proud of that place when I was first able to rent those rooms on the top floor of the tallest building in the town we lived in then—the apartment upstairs on the top floor of the very same building where the law office was down on the second floor, just above the bank—bringing Mother home to our new place for the first time, both of us so excited about how close it was to the office and to the courthouse just across the street, to the grocery store and what would be the boys' school, just blocks away, and you could see clear over the tops of the magnolia trees on the court square, all three blocks out to the edges of town. But then, after Deed died, being there was more painful than either of us could bear. Our steps were always slowing down instead of speeding up as we headed up the stairs to home. When coming home makes the ones you love cringe in pain, it's time to get out of there.

And that's when we decided to move to Bumblebee. No sidewalks. Nothing hard to land on if you fell. No buildings to speak of more than a single story high. No high windows anywhere you could see to fall out of. And it had fields, and woods, and places I could take the boys hunting and fishing, and we could grow a garden—and this at a time when things were starting to get mighty tight. Not just for us, but for everybody, and from what everyone was saying, the Depression was only going to get worse. So, Mother and I talked about it. And we prayed about it. And then, just before it was time for Gent to start to school, we moved.

1.4 NASHVILLE, 2014

PROBITY

I grew up within spitting distance of a tiny speck-in-the-road known as Bumblebee. It always seemed to me that a more accurate name would've been Honeybee, since the name referred to the millions of inhabitants of a nearby three-acre stand of woods that burned down long before the town sprung up. The forest had grown back, eventually, so that by the time I came along there was new growth scattered in among the ancient tree trunks still standing where they had once reigned majestically over what became the town. Everyone from miles around went to those woods to gather their honey from the hives hidden in the charred and hollowed-out tree carcasses, or else they bought their honey from someone else, who did. Anyway, the name of the town had been decided on a lifetime before I was born and I never did find out why. Maybe it was because whoever decided knew something it took me a long time to figure out for myself: few honeybees that sting someone live to sting again, but any old bumblebee can wound you more than once. Honeybee, it wasn't; Bumblebee, it was.

Bumblebee was located somewhere between ten and fifteen minutes west of the river, depending on how fast you drove, and a little over half an hour north of Nashville, Tennessee. Bumblebee was unincorporated, of course. It said so, right there on the two signs posted on opposing sides of the same pole, just out in front of the post office. The post office itself was about as big as most people's kitchens. Just enough room for two people to squeeze in out of the rain and hold a conversation while checking their mail, if they liked each other well enough. *Bumblebee, unincorporated. Population 1,634.* Bumblebee was so small that by the time you realized you were there, you were already headed out of town.

The most important thing about Bumblebee, if you were from there, was that it was south of the Mason-Dixon Line. If you're from north of the line, that likely doesn't mean much to you; but if you're from the south of it, it means everything. It means you've been carrying a chip on your shoulder ever since The Recent Unpleasantness, even if you hadn't been born yet then. Bumblebee seems, even now, like such an insignificant place you'd never believe anything important could have ever happened there.

But if you thought that, you'd be wrong.

THE BUREAUCRAT

The experiments kept going awry. I had started working for The Company in the mid '40s, and the goal of our division was to create a perfect spy, someone who could be tortured endlessly without ever giving up a single secret. It wasn't working.

In years to come our researchers would make a number of contributions to the popular culture such as making LSD a household name—a side effect of our work to develop a drug that could make a man forget secrets at will—but back in those days, our focus was on developing multiple personalities within a single individual. The theory was that when exposed to the correct stimuli, a subject's mind could be forced to fragment. This fragmentation would create a number of separate personalities, one or more of which could then be trained as a spy, with that one particular fragment being accessible only to the individuals who created it. Anyone else who questioned or tortured the subject in an attempt to gain information would only have access to the parts of the personality we wanted them to be able to access. Our information would be safe.

We knew the phenomenon of multiple personalities had been described at least as early as 1810, when the first known case history of a subject with the disorder—a woman named Mary Reynolds—was documented.

Slightly over a century later, in 1930, George Estabrooks had the right idea—though he didn't carry it far enough—when he theorized that hypnotism could create a new identity that would be a perfect spy. Estabrooks' theory was close, but hypnotism wasn't quite powerful enough to create Multiple Personality Disorder either. By that time, as you probably know, we usually referred to it as MPD.

Two decades after Estabrooks posited his theory, Shirley Jackson's research before writing her short story "The Lottery" in 1948 and then her novel *The Bird's Nest* in 1954 resulted in stories so powerfully constructed they convinced many of her readers that adults with MPD could, in fact, be created whenever there were sufficient acts of emotional trauma, physical violence, or sexual assault as their foundation. Ms. Jackson's research was focused on the premise under which my group was already operating.

1.6 NASHVILLE, 2014

Probity

Most folks around Bumblebee were farmers, but my granddaddy was a real estate lawyer so all his children and grandchildren got names a real estate lawyer would like. My older brother Ernie was named Earnest for earnest money. My little sister's Equity. I got lucky when they decided to call me Probity, which was the name of the law office. My granddaddy used to always grin at me and say, "Little Bit," he'd say, "a name like that calls for a lifetime of unimpeachable integrity." That always made me feel mighty proud. I've been trying to live up to it—and to him and my grandmomma—ever since.

I won't even *tell* you what my baby brother was named. Only my mother calls him that. All the rest of us have always just called him Brother, because his name was so potentially embarrassing if you went in your mind where Ernie and I had gone with nicknames, giggling, out in the backyard, right after he was born. After we got over it being so funny, we realized we oughtn't do that to anybody, so we never called him by his real name again.

My father's name was Contingency. I dearly loved my grandparents, but who names their kid something like that, seriously? Almost everybody just called him Gen or Gent, which was infinitely better than a lot of nicknames he could have been given. Gent Jones.

The law office served homeowners and home buyers around and south of Bumblebee, in Davidson

County or Nashville, mostly, the outskirts of which weren't too far from the crossroads where Bumblebee would've been marked on the map, if only it'd been big enough. Granddaddy couldn't get work doing any fancy kind of law that paid a lot of money in Nashville, but that's another story altogether, having to do with Republicans and Democrats, and, like I said, living south of the Mason-Dixon Line. But anyway, it's why we all lived in Bumblebee, where it was cheaper, and why he made his living doing property searches, writing up real estate contracts, and managing escrow accounts. That sort of thing. I don't remember any real estate agents hanging around, so maybe they didn't even have any back then, but who knows? I guess there could've been. My memory of that time is not all that great.

Grandmomma worked with Granddaddy at Probity Law starting when Gent hit grade school. She didn't have any other kids left at home after that, because it was after her baby boy, my Uncle Deed, died. By the time I got to high school, she'd started in her seventies at the YMCA Night Law School in Nashville, hoping to get to be a lawyer, too, but then she died not long after Granddaddy did, in 1971. She didn't make it long enough for her graduation, or mine either, that next spring, and I always felt bad about that. She was a pistol, my grandmomma was. Golly, I miss her. Granddaddy, too.

I've never missed Gent much, and he's mostly who this story is about: how he got to be the way he was, and why it was he did what he did. Funny, isn't it, that I'd be compelled to tell the story of someone I didn't much like? But I just can't get him out of my mind. All those things that happened just keep going round, and round, and round inside of my skull, and I just keep hoping that maybe, if I can get them out of there, maybe then he'll finally leave me alone.

1.7 REMEMBERING BUMBLEBEE, 1933

GENT

We were poor when I was young; so poor, in fact, that for a number of years when Mother fixed our plates, she used to tell us she'd already eaten all she wanted while she was cooking. I didn't realize till years later that the truth was, she never even ate those meals at all—because if she had, there'd have been less food for her to feed to Daddy and the rest of us. I don't know why I didn't see it then. Couldn't see beyond myself, I guess. That, or I was too trusting, because if she said it, it must have been so. I wanted it to have been so. Needed it, even. Then there were other times, I realize now, when there was nothing at all to eat but the walnuts or mushrooms she sent us to find out in the woods. But we never knew that then. We thought it was an adventure, the way she made it sound like we were being pioneers or pirates, but the truth is, there just wasn't anything left for Daddy or anyone else to shoot or catch or for us to pick or dig up. Daddy worked hard in the garden when there wasn't legal work for him to catch up on, and taught us how to work it, too, but sometimes even the garden ran out because there wasn't rain, or there was too much of it, or the insects and animals got to it first—and then we went hungry after all. I swore to myself I'd never let *my* family want for anything once I was grown.

Daddy had a hard time getting work because he was the only lawyer for miles around who was brave enough to admit he was a Republican living in a Democratic county. He wouldn't deny it because it was true, and denying the truth would've meant denying himself and who he was, which is how he ended up doing real estate work in the first place. I guess even a bunch of damn Democrats trusted him enough to have him look up a title search and write a contract for selling or buying a piece of property, even when they wouldn't hire him to do something that would pay just enough more to make it possible for him to pay the note and feed and clothe us kids and keep his pride. It still makes me mad when I think about it.

When I wanted piano lessons, God help me, Daddy and Mother didn't have any way to pay for those either, so Mother went and talked to the only piano teacher around, who traded teaching me piano for Mother doing her laundry and house-cleaning. When I got old enough to go to school and Mother started working with Daddy at the law office, she didn't have time to do someone else's laundry as well as our own, so I traded the piano teacher myself, doing her chores for lessons instead. Why I wanted those lessons so badly, I don't know, but it was something to keep my mind off Deed, and it seemed I just couldn't stop thinking about him being dead. Thinking about him made me sad and mad, made me want to hit somebody and hurt them real bad.

And sometimes, I did.

1.8 NASHVILLE, 2014

PROBITY

My mama's sister, my Aunt Leenie, she's always said Gent was the meanest man she ever met, and that he treated me worse than anybody, but she didn't know why. She told me the story about the time they all went swimming at the lake at least a million times, how Gent drug me out into the lake—I was just about two or three, or I guess I might've even been four years old by then—and he held me there in the water, screaming, crying, begging him to take me back to land 'til my lips and skin were blue and my teeth were chattering so hard she could hear them all the way up on the bank, knocking against each other so. And how when he finally took me back to land, he wouldn't let anybody be nice to me or put their arms around me to get me warm or wrap me in a towel, and made me stand there for who knows how long 'til I finally stopped shivering and crying, because I'd been bad and hadn't done what he'd said—which was to let go of him and swim— when I was too scared to let go because the water was dark and you couldn't even begin to guess what was in there, and besides, I didn't know how to swim, anyway.

I don't remember it. There's a lot about my childhood I still don't remember, even now. For the longest time I didn't want to remember anything, but then when my own Little Boy was about the age I was then, I started remembering and once I started, I couldn't stop, even though I wanted to more dearly than I ever wanted anything before or since in my whole life. But it was like a crack in a dam, or opening a floodgate. Once the memories started coming, I couldn't push them back or stop them no matter how hard I tried, and for the longest time, it seemed, each new one was worse than the one before.

1.9 BUMBLEBEE, 1934

GRANDMOMMA

We never could get through to Gent after Deed died. Si was eleven at the time and Gent was not quite five, and after that it was as though he was brittle, like something fragile had broken inside of him.

On the outside, he was still just as cute as ever. He had the looks he must have gotten from my side of the family—dark skin, jet black hair, deep brown eyes, sharp cheekbones, almost cavernous dimples at the outer edges of his smile, and a dent the size of a crater right in the middle of his chin. I thought he looked completely irresistible, but inside, he just never could believe anyone else saw him as good-looking, or strong, or smart, or anything else that was good in any way. He would complain to us that he was ugly compared to Si, who got his daddy's blond hair and blue eyes and shot up by the time he was twelve to be taller than anyone else in the family. He'd say everyone liked Si better than they liked him, which wasn't true, though Si certainly was easier to get along with than Gent ever was. He was like the little girl in the poem, the one with the curl in the middle of her forehead: When Gent was good, he was very, very good, but when Gent was bad, he was horrid.

When he *was* being good, though, Gent was so charming no one could resist him. On those days, you could tell he was still feeling bad about Deed, and Daddy and I wanted to be able to give him anything he wanted and everything he asked for, always hoping something would get through to ease that hurt we could see pounding inside him. But nothing ever seemed to, and when he was angry, dark clouds would hover over him, and everyone around walked on eggshells if he was in the room, and we all tried to stay at least an arm's length away.

1.10 SENATE SELECT COMMITTEE TRANSCRIPT
WASHINGTON, 1975

THE BUREAUCRAT

You've got to remember that by 1947 the Cold War was in full bloom. It still is, of course, even though now it is obviously under the rug—but pretending that it's over doesn't make it so. The Chinese had clearly developed something that we couldn't duplicate. Prisoners of war who passed through Manchuria inexplicably "lost" time, and no one knew what their interrogators were doing, or how. The same thing was happening in Korea. And then who knew what the Soviets were up to? But Americans couldn't reliably reproduce the same results, no matter what we tried.

Eventually we were able to gather a fair amount of anecdotal support for the theory that the minds of some children would instinctively splinter after exposure to traumatic stimuli, compartmentalizing parts of the child's experience that were too overwhelming for them to remember. This was more prevalent the brighter they were.

The problem was that none of us could figure out how to make the same thing happen to willing adults. While traumatized *children* instinctively developed multiple personalities which could be "triggered" to switch from one personality to another, each with its own set of memories and experiences, *adults* subjected to the same kinds of traumatic events reacted differently. They might develop amnesia to certain events, or recurrent nightmares or terrors, but they didn't readily split into separate personalities the same way children did. It was most inconvenient.

1.11 REMEMBERING BUMBLEBEE, 1935

GENT

I remember, too, the day when I was nine, when Daddy took us fishing down at the bend in the river where the water was dark and smooth, and everyone who lived nearby knew underneath the surface the current was dangerous and fast. Daddy and I were planning on going by ourselves, just the two of us, but then when it was time to leave Si woke up and wanted to go, too, and so did Si's friend, Bobby, who had spent the night. And Bobby's stupid hound dog Boomer followed us.

We'd gone before the break of day, of course. Daddy always did like going places before it was first light, especially if it was to go fishing. The water was a silver slash through the night with the reflection of the new moon glinting across it, just about the only thing we could see in the dark.

We'd been out there a while, and I was running through worms like nobody's business, but I wasn't having any luck bringing anything to the shore. And Bobby just *wouldn't* shut up about it. "I got one! I got one!" he kept whispering loud enough that everyone could hear him, every time he got a nibble. "Did you get one yet? I've got five already... how about you? I got another one! Did you get one yet?"

Every time he said anything, I felt worse. It should have been a wonderful morning. Quiet. Just a little fog. Almost silent except for the sounds of the birds waking up and the crickets making their presence known to each other and the occasional splash of a fish or a frog or a turtle far out in the water or sometimes right up next to the bank. There should have been no one out there but Daddy and me, just the two of us.

But Bobby and Boomer and Si were there and Bobby just wouldn't shut up. He *wouldn't*. So I grabbed my worms and my pole and left all three of them there with Daddy, and hiked downstream following the shoreline around the bend, mostly out of eyesight and earshot, because of the bushes and trees. But I could *still* hear Bobby's whispering floating out across the water.

I couldn't get away no matter what I did. I couldn't get away from them out on that creek bank. I couldn't get away from Deed inside my head. I couldn't get away anywhere I went. I was trapped, and there was nowhere I could go. I tore my shirt collar open because I couldn't breathe. I couldn't get away. There was *nowhere* I could go.

Then that *stupid* Boomer came running up, jumping and licking until he knocked me down and all my worms spilled out onto the ground, and it wasn't light enough to find them even with my nose six inches from the dirt and I was running out of them anyway, and I got madder and madder at everybody and everything, and Boomer was running in circles around me like it was a game, and he wouldn't stop until one time when I went to push him away instead I grabbed him by the neck and started choking him and choking him until he made some funny little sounds and started squirming and tried to get away and then I choked him harder until he stopped moving at all, and then I pushed him out into the water as far as I could with my pole and tried to push him under the surface so the current would take him where no one would know what I did, and I didn't make a sound or say anything to anyone until his body had floated far enough downstream that I couldn't see it anymore.

And then everything was still.

CHAPTER TWO

2.1 NASHVILLE, 2014

PROBITY

The story I always heard growing up was that Gent grew up feeling like a failure. Everybody always talked about how he had an older brother, my Uncle Si, who was just about darn near perfect, and how he had a baby brother who was cute and cuddly and died, and Gent was just—well—Gent.

He was in the middle. Like me.

I've got an older brother my mama dotes on, too, and a younger sister who's darn near perfect. I even have a baby brother who was cute and cuddly 'til he grew out of it. So why didn't Gent like me?

He never worked hard enough at school. Me, neither. He didn't have many friends. Neither did I. And he believed his mama and his daddy didn't pay as much attention to him as he thought they ought to. I felt that way sometimes, too.

I like to think about religion and psychology and stuff, and I know he did, too. And neither one of us could see worth a toot.

So, what I couldn't ever figure out was why he didn't like me any more than he did, when we had so much in common. Or if he *did* like me, why couldn't he act like he did? I just couldn't figure out what I had done that made him hate me so much he'd do all that stuff to me and all those others he didn't even know. I spent years trying to make it make sense.

2.2 REMEMBERING BUMBLEBEE, 1936

GENT

When I was in the fourth grade, somebody finally figured out I needed glasses, but even then, it wasn't Mother or Daddy who realized it. They were still too wrapped up in Si and the memory of Deed, and never did pay much attention to me. It's hard to believe it took *anyone* that long to notice, though, because it turned out I was blind as a bat. You'd think someone would have picked up on it before then, but no one did until my fourth-grade class went for a routine vision screening—you know, the one where you stand behind the line and they show you the big "E" and see how many lines you can read underneath it, except I couldn't even tell it was an "E." They said I was "wall-eyed," too, which meant that unlike folks who are cross-eyed, my eyes focused out at the walls.

Well into adulthood, I was still using the torturous device I had to start using then, one end of which looked like binoculars and was held by the left hand snug against the nose. From that piece, a rod extended almost arm's length, where a card showing two separate images of the same thing—something like a visual stereo—was held by the right hand. The card with the images on it slid in and out like a trombone, closer and farther from the eyes, exercising the muscles surrounding the eyes as they worked to keep the images in focus. I hated that stereoscope, but not as much as I hated wearing glasses. I wasn't very good-looking anyway, especially compared with Si, who was seven years older, and my glasses were as thick as milk bottle bottoms. Si was smarter and stronger, and all of my teachers remembered him after having him first.

His was a legacy with which I was always being unfavorably compared.

2.3 BUMBLEBEE, 1938

UNCLE SI

Gent was always trying to get out of trouble by blaming what he did on someone else. You'd think he'd been born with a halo, the way he tried to present himself, but it was just an illusion. He was no angel.

I was already in the second grade when he was born, and no sooner than he could talk he'd blame things on me, even if I wasn't at home. "Si did it." "Si told me to." "Si made me do it." "Si was *thinking* about doing it, so I had to."

Most of my friends' little brothers and sisters were annoying, but Gent took it to a whole different level. Sometimes, it seemed as though he would do things there was no other reason to do than just so he *could* blame them on me. He was forever trying to get other people to do his homework, or his chores, or give him something. If he *didn't* do something, well, that was usually blamed on me, too. "Si said *he* was going to take out the trash," or, "I thought *Si* would feed the dog."

And usually, he got away with it.

No one besides Gent and me knew what really happened the day Deed died, but everyone who blamed me felt sorry for Gent afterwards because he was never quite right after that. He knew, and I knew, and as far as I know, to this day we were the only people who ever did. He begged me not to tell, and I promised I wouldn't, ever. And I never have.

All I can tell you is that it is impossible to make someone who is four years old mind you if they are determined not to. As he got older, he just got worse. And after I went into the service? Well, there was no controlling him then.

2.4 SENATE SELECT COMMITTEE TRANSCRIPT
WASHINGTON, 1975

THE BUREAUCRAT

We believed that the trauma our team was producing wasn't severe enough to be successful, but we kept running into problems there, too. If the thing that pushed children over the edge was the fear that they might actually be killed, the only way to reproduce that fear in adults was to convince our subjects that some of them had actually been terminated in the presence of others. To do that, we needed not only subjects but also staff we could control completely and trust absolutely to be discreet. There were a few experts in fields such as psychology and psychiatry who were eager to take on the assignment—most notably doctors from among the fifteen hundred German scientists we rehabilitated during Project Paperclip after World War II. These were Nazi scientists with skills and knowledge the U.S. wanted badly enough to circumvent the war crimes tribunal and bring here, thus assuring that no other country could make use of them. Even so, there weren't enough with the right skills and attitude to staff the program in a way that ensured results.

The problem was that too many of our employees had scruples that interfered with the successful completion of our experiments. No matter what promises we made regarding security and confidentiality, the percentage of staff who believed that what we proposed to do was simply *wrong* was large.

While some admitted this under questioning, there were others about whom we merely suspected this was true, based on criteria such as church attendance and personality testing. None of this group could be trusted to participate. The second group included those who were apparently willing to follow orders, but who were clearly afraid of being prosecuted if information regarding our research methodology ever became public. These staff members as well, were suspect. Since both groups knew that every step of the process was being monitored and recorded and there were more than a few staff members in each group who knew that some of our Paperclip assets had been in danger of being prosecuted for war crimes before being recruited into our program—and I suppose some of them had figured out that our peace-time research might be construed as falling into that category as well—the challenges of ensuring a successful clinical trial were enormous.

2.5 BUMBLEBEE, 1938

GRANDMOMMA

Gent was almost old enough to graduate from
Bumblebee's grade school to the county schools before I
found out that the other kids in his class were teasing
him mercilessly. I'd never have found out at all, except
the mother of one of his classmates took it upon herself
to tell me what was happening.

By that time, Gent was agonizingly shy, self-
conscious about his looks and his thick glasses, and
painfully awkward at any school sport. He'd always
been the last one picked for any team, if at all, and it
seemed what he liked best about the piano was that he
didn't have to interact with anyone else to play it. A lot
of the time, he didn't even practice at all. He'd just go
in the parlor where the piano was and lean his head on
it and daydream, or sit there on the bench, poking at
the keys.

Then, when Gent was in the sixth grade, one of his
classmates told his mother that he didn't want to play
with Gent 'cause nobody liked him. When she asked
her son to tell her more, he said it was embarrassing to
be seen with Gent 'cause everyone made fun of him,
girls didn't like him, and he was a sissy. Then he said
Gent hung out with the kids from the other side of the
tracks.

I knew exactly what that meant. Bumblebee was so
small there was only one school for all the white kids in
grade school and another school for the children of

color. "The other side of the tracks" was just what it said. The railroad ran through town, with white folks living on one side of the tracks, and colored folks living on the other. The school they all went to, from first grade on up, was on the other side of the tracks from where we lived and our children went to school. Our school only went through eighth grade, so white kids from our side of the tracks went in to the county seat for high school, with all the other white kids from the county. The school on the other side of the tracks was all the colored children had.

There was a gully that ran along the tracks, and between the tracks and the gully, well, that line pretty much delineated the races.

Oh, some folks from that side came over to ours to do yard work, or work in kitchens or fields, or do housework, and sometimes they brought their children with them. A few would go to the stores in the county seat, which was past Bumblebee on our side of the tracks. And every once in a while, the doctor would make a trip to the other side. But those were the exceptions rather than the rule.

The gully on our side of the tracks ran along the property line at the boundary of our backyard, and sometimes Gent talked to and made friends with kids he could see on the other side of the tracks from our yard. Si was so much older he didn't want to play with Gent much, so in the beginning Gent would yell across the gully and the tracks at the kids on the other side, and they'd yell back, and eventually, as kids on our side played with him less and less, he and a few of the kids from the other side started playing together in the gully. They'd pick up the shiny glass slag they found hidden in amongst the gravel that lined the tracks, and there was one little boy, Billy, with whom Gent made pretty good friends. They drifted apart for a while, though, when Gent was in high school, and I never did find out if they had a falling out or if it was just that normal drifting apart that happens when children end up at different schools.

I sat down with Gent that night and told him what his classmate had said to his mother. Then I told him that he had plenty of sense, and that I trusted him to make his own decisions about who he wanted to play with... and then I told him that every decision he made in his life should be an informed decision. What other people thought should never make him change his mind one way or the other, but he ought to make his decisions knowing what other people were thinking and saying, and why.

2.6 Remembering Bumblebee, 1940

Gent

The United States is hopelessly outdated and naively provincial in its moral attitudes regarding sex and sexuality, and the harm we do by imposing these unrealistic expectations on our youth should be criminalized. Take your average eighth grader. By the time he gets to eighth grade, your average youth has been brainwashed into believing not that he is special, but that there is something wrong with him.

You know how it goes, at a certain age the hormones start raging, and as Mother used to say, we start "noticing" each other. She would say boys notice girls; girls notice boys. You start noticing the same person everywhere you go, someone you never noticed there before. This boy never paid any attention to the fact that he passed that particular girl's house on the way to the store, until one day, he *noticed* her. She'd never really *noticed* he went to her church, until one day, there he was. Except that isn't how it is with our more cosmopolitan youth—the girls noticing boys and boys noticing girls part. Girls and boys who are not from such narrow-minded provinces notice each other in virtually unlimited variety and form.

The institution of the American gym class is among the worst. For most of the school day, a boy can hold his books in front of himself and hide his emotions, but in gym class there is no such escape. Shorts and tee-shirts don't hide much, and God help us, even worse, there are the locker rooms where boys are required to dress before and after class, with the shower facilities they are expected to make use of afterwards. Before gym isn't usually so bad, but after? There is no hiding in a locker room. And no red-blooded American boy should be required to keep his eyes where society says they ought to be: on the floor, on the lockers—anywhere away from the attributes of the other guys. The truly free thinkers not only compare themselves to their peers, like everyone else does, but also have feelings for them that convention demands should leave them reeling in shame. Pity the boys who have difficulty controlling their physical responses. In an environment in which the popular guys are slapping each other on their asses and shoving each other around, laughing, hot and sweaty, those who are not so popular or are differently inclined are laughed at, humiliated, and demeaned, or worse. Be sure each forward thinker fears anyone else knowing what is going on inside his head, and believes he is the only one who feels that way.

I knew it. And I knew Si wouldn't have felt that way. Not at my age. Not ever.

2.7 BUMBLEBEE, 1941

GRANDDADDY

While at Gent's age all I could think about was girls, music seemed to be the only thing that held any interest for him. By his fifteenth birthday in May of '41, our financial situation had improved enough that Mother and I decided we wanted to take him on the new Washington-to-Memphis train to hear Ignacy Jan Paderewski, who was eighty years old that summer, perform in what turned out to be his final U.S. tour. The concert we attended was one of his last; he died just a few months later.

The Tennessean was a new train at the time, and had only been in service a couple of months. It ran through Nashville, and one of the cities on Paderewski's tour was on the route. Mother and I were eager to take a ride on it. Gent had been practicing some on the piano, though not as much as we thought the cost of his lessons warranted, and we were hoping to inspire him to work harder at his music by taking him to hear one of the most famous pianists in the world. With Si in the service, the trip promised to be a great opportunity for the three of us to have some time together, giving Gent some of the individual attention he constantly wanted.

The Tennessean had Pullman sleeper cars, so we were going to ride out in a regular passenger car, eat lunch in the dining car on the way, attend the matinee afternoon performance, have dinner, and then catch the next train back, sleeping all the way home. We'd be back at Union Station in Nashville in time for breakfast.

Gent was so excited he talked all the way there and most of the way home, and Mother and I laughed later that we'd have saved money by skipping the Pullman car altogether—no more than we slept, we could have done almost as well in our seats. But it was worth it. It was a day when Gent seemed truly happy, which was all we ever wanted for him.

After we got home, Mother and I couldn't help noticing that Gent didn't seem to be as impressed with the way Paderewski played as he was by the way the man acted and was treated. He couldn't stop talking about the fact that Paderewski wore not just a suit or a tuxedo, but formal tails, with shiny, black patent leather shoes that gleamed all the way up to where we were sitting in the upper balcony. He talked about the casual-yet-practiced way Paderewski flipped his tails over the back of his padded bench and adjusted it to the exact height he wanted it as he sat down; the way his hands flew and danced over the keyboard; the wave upon wave of applause that flowed over him, and his gracious acceptance of it; and the length of the line of admirers waiting after the performance for just a moment, a handshake, a word with the great man himself.

That's what Gent was impressed with. We had gone to hear one of the best musicians in the world, but he came home impressed not with the *performance*, but with the *show*.

2.8 Remembering Bumblebee, 1942

Gent

It wasn't until high school that I finally found a niche of sorts. Well, two of them, actually, which between them comprised my entire social circle. The piano, a solitary instrument, hardly counted for that purpose, but the two social outlets I eventually found were related to it by virtue of being other performing arts. The first release I discovered was speech; the second, band.

Drama, forensics, improvisation, debate… with all of its various manifestations, speech was a magnificent liberation for someone like me. For a boy who had spent most of every day of his life up until then pretending to be someone he was not, trying to fit in, trying to appear as a self others would admire (or at least refrain from humiliating), it was glorious. The class offered at the county high school was different from anything else I had studied up till that point, and seemed tailor-made for me: it provided an opportunity to be rewarded for publicly acting as though I were someone other than the persona I wore the majority of the time.

It was there I learned to stand on a stage and be unafraid; to speak off the cuff; to roll with the punches, whether physical or verbal, without losing my footing; to wear other roles like a change of clothes I donned or discarded at my pleasure. The fact that I was praised for pretending to be all manner of persons other than myself without censure was good practice for later in life, and the benefit of getting to be with other, shall we say, "dramatically inclined" young men was the icing on the cake. My goodness, it opened a whole new world to my tentative approaches.

In band, I played the flute because it was the only instrument other than the piano to which our family, still struggling somewhat financially, had access. The particular instrument I had at my disposal had already been handed down a couple of times, but for the time being, at least, it was mine. Most of the other flautists were girls, but there wasn't anything I could do about that. The flute was the only instrument I had, so once again, in order to belong to the group at large, I was the odd one out. Still, though, band offered an opportunity to be a part of a community that came together to create something larger than any of us could create individually.

In both band and speech, I was provided with a fascinating juxtaposition of a stage which served as a vehicle for my being rewarded for being a "star" (or at least one of them), while at the same time netting me the reward of blessed anonymity. In the first case, band, I was anonymous because I was only one part of the whole; in the second case, speech, I was anonymous because I could hide behind a face which was not my own. In each case, performing allowed me to escape for at least a little while from being who I was. As a very small-town fish in the much larger pond of high school, performing arts became my refuge.

It was almost like I wasn't there at all.

THE BUREAUCRAT

For a while we went back to the drawing board in trying to figure out how MPD was created, using children to whom we had easy access as research subjects. Primarily, these were children in daycares on military bases or in institutions, but even there we had to be careful. Too much trauma or not enough, and we couldn't be sure the kids would keep quiet about what was going on. Still, they were easier to manipulate than adults.

We found out early on that all we had to do was kill a few puppies in front of them, and it was easy enough to convince them the same thing would happen to them if they told. Threaten to send a parent to the front line somewhere, and a child could be convinced to do almost anything. On a military base or in an institution, it was easy to convince a child that someone was watching everything they said or did, or even thought. But at the end of the day, no matter what regimen we came up with, no one could predictably and controllably get volunteer personalities to split, and that was what we needed. By the time we figured out the answer, it was almost embarrassingly simple.

CHAPTER THREE

3.1 REMEMBERING BUMBLEBEE, 1944

GENT

Si inherited Daddy's height, great vision, and good looks, while I inherited Mother's short stature, bad eyes, and dark complexion—and there is nothing any of us can do about what we inherit. Being older, Si was always bigger than I was, smarter than I was, better at everything. He was taller and stronger, so he played basketball and every other sport better than I could. He was better looking, and had all the girls keening over him, while no one at all was keening over me. When he got old enough to enlist, he came back a war hero; by the time my group came up, because of my terrible eyesight all I got was a 4F. There was nothing *I* could do to be a hero, and it wasn't my fault. None of it was.

Well, okay, the truth is, most of it really was Mother's and Daddy's faults, though some of it was Si's and Deed's. Everyone thought Deed was so adorable, and his life had been cut short, and wasn't it *sad*. Si was so *perfect*, being tall and handsome and strong and smart. If Mother and Daddy hadn't been so wrapped up in grieving for Deed and doting on Si, they'd have had more time for me. And if they hadn't been all-consumed by always trying to do the right thing, trying never to hurt anybody or anything, by being so kind and easygoing and *wounded*, they'd have had time to make *me* into a man, too. They'd have taught me better, made me study, made me practice, *made* me be more disciplined. It wasn't my fault they let me get away with everything. *They* made me lazy by just not caring enough to make me work harder. As graduation approached, it seemed my whole senior class was moving on to do what they were going to do the rest of their lives, while I had absolutely no idea. The only thing I could do even halfway decently was play the piano.

By that time, I'd moved up to a piano teacher in Nashville who understood our financial situation and encouraged me to apply to an endowed music school in Philadelphia. If I could get in, I'd be on scholarship just like every other student there, which would be the only way I'd ever be able to go anywhere. So I rode the train up to Philly all by myself and auditioned, and sure enough, I did get in, eventually; but even then it was not because I was good enough, but because they'd already accepted all the students they really wanted that year and still had one slot left. I found out later they only chose me to fill out the class because I was different from all the other students they accepted that year, all of whom had grown up in better homes, lived in better towns, went to better schools, and had better teachers than I did. They chose me because I was different. Not good. *Different.* Interesting, they said. They said I had potential. It was what we called in Bumblebee a "backhanded compliment." You know, like, "You don't sweat much for a fat girl." It sounded like it might have been a nice thing to say, but everybody knew it was really a slam.

I got into a school that everyone knew was one of the best in the world, but everybody *at* the school knew I was the worst one there.

3.2 INTERLOCHEN, 1944

THE FIRST

I still get a little thrill every time I think about the summer I spent with Contingency Jones. We were both so much younger then. He was hovering on the cusp of manhood, while I was slightly more, well, *seasoned*, because I remember it was my last summer at Oberlin and the summer after he graduated from high school, only a couple of months before he started college. He'd come up from Nashville for the National Music Camp at Interlochen. I was working as a camp counselor for the summer because the Director of Bands at Oberlin, where I was going to be a senior that year, was conducting. Mr. Williams knew I needed the money and got me the job, but if he hadn't paid me one thin dime and I had worked my fingers to the *bone*, honey, it would *still* have been worth it! That time with Connie has been more precious to me in my life than *any* amount of money that could ever have passed through my pockets.

Oh, my! He was simply *delicious!* He may not have thought so at the time, but I could see it right away. He was trying so hard to act sophisticated, with no idea how to pull *that* off, and he was trying to look butch, too, but then, honey, every man was trying to look butch in those days. His parents had borrowed the money to send him to Interlochen so he could immerse himself in music before he left home at the end of the summer, and up until that summer he had never been with anyone. Ever. In his whole life. That boy was ripe for the picking. My, oh *my*, was he ripe. And he *wanted* to be picked, too! I was happy to be the one who did, not long after we met.

I had already received my initiation, getting my early education at my daddy's knee, as it were, so *I* knew quite a bit about what's what, and I'd been around the block enough times by then that I'd learned how to pick up on most of the signals. The signals I was looking for were *easy* to pick up from Connie, honey. That boy was simply *radiating* them. And I wasn't mistaken. When I made my approach, he welcomed me with open arms.

After camp ended, he went back to that small town he was from to get ready for school, and I thought that was the end of it until I unexpectedly saw him again during the third week of September. It was 1944, and I remember that it was a Friday night and *Of Mice and Men* was showing at the Allen Art Little Theater right there on campus. I simply couldn't *wait* to see it, to find out how they presented the relationship between the two main characters, but as I left the dorm on my way to the theater, I heard my name called out, turned around, and suddenly, *there! he! was!* That small-town boy had only been away from home for a few weeks, and he was *already* so lonely he had figured out how to take the train to Cleveland, and then the bus from Cleveland to Oberlin. I'm sure you can understand that we missed the movie completely. He stayed through the next day, Saturday, when there was a dance at the Rec Hall with the Navy Band playing. They were simply *divine*, honey, and *not* to be missed, so as you would expect, we went! Oberlin was co-ed even then, so there were plenty of dance partners to choose from, and Connie had learned to dance *oh! so! wonderfully!* when he had performed in Gershwin's *Girl Crazy* his junior year in high school. Oh, how I *loved* to watch that boy dance!

On Sunday, I rode the bus with him to Cleveland, where I could hardly *bear* to put him back on the train, but he had to be back at school in time for classes on Monday. It was just too wonderful! That Connie sure knew how to make a 'girl' feel special. He should have spent the entire weekend practicing, but instead, he spent it with *me*.

3.3 NASHVILLE, 2014

PROBITY

When I was just a kid, I read everything I could get my hands on. Time spent reading about somebody else was time I could escape from feeling bad, deep-down inside myself.

You'd think it was because when I was reading I didn't have to be who I was. I could go anywhere. I could be anyone. I could do anything. You'd think any time I spent reading was time I didn't have to live inside of my own skin.

But I don't really remember that being the case back then. I don't remember ever imagining I *was* somebody else, somewhere else, doing something else. I just remember that as long as I was reading I wasn't in the here-and-now. Any time I was thinking about something else, I didn't have to feel what it was to be *me.* Reading, I was distracted from feeling anything at all that I can remember. And whenever I was reading, I was learning about something. Golly, I loved to learn.

Sometimes I think Gent must've wanted to get out of his skin, too. I can't be sure, of course. Most of what I've put together about his life is just guessing. But the little parts I remember or can put together, well, they make me think that.

I remember him saying more than once that at one time or another he had read "just enough books about psychology," as he put it, "to be dangerous." Now why would you say something like that, unless you *wanted* to be dangerous? Or maybe at least to appear to be?

I don't know enough about psychology to know anything for sure, especially not where the answer to that one lies, but I do know right where his psychology *books* were. While we lived at the farmhouse, he had a chair in our library that was just his. No one else was supposed to even sit in it, but sometimes I used to sneak in there when he wasn't at home. His was the best chair in the room for reading, because all the others were hard and wood and were gathered around the table, but that one was great big, covered with brown corduroy, stuffed full of something soft, and sat all by itself at the other end of the room close to the door to the hall. And if you were sitting in his chair there was a lampstand just behind your right shoulder between the chair and the shelves on that side of the room, and on the shelf just *right there*, just at his right hand, those were the most interesting books in the room.

Oh, we had lots of other books, and I'd read almost all of them more than once. There were novels. There were history books and geography books. There were books about poetry, the rules for playing all sorts of games, music books, and books about medical stuff and first aid. There were even books about math and science, real people living and dead, and encyclopedias. Oh, my goodness, I loved those encyclopedias.

But *those* books, the ones on the shelves just even with and below your eyes if you were sitting in his chair, right where you could reach out and touch them without ever getting up, those were the books about magic. About religion. About psychology. About the occult. About *sex*.

3.4 REMEMBERING PHILADELPHIA, 1945

GENT

Ah, to be as young and naive again as I was during those first few days in Philadelphia, when everything—it seemed in the entire world—was new and wonderful, and I had not yet come face to face with either the person I already was or the person I was destined from before my birth to become. In those early days, I met men and women the likes of whom I'd never come in contact with before, students and teachers even more remarkable than the ones I had met the previous summer at Interlochen—and they, of course, had been the most amazing collection of individuals I had ever encountered till then.

Among those I met that first few days were Walter and Theodore, who would become my best friends during my college years. Walt, a violinist, and Theo, a fellow pianist, were both just beginning their second year as I began my first. Walt was a couple of years younger than most of his class, so he comfortably fit in with the newcomers—and he knew everything about everyone at the school, whether janitor, student, or professor. He was a veritable fount of information regarding all things school-related, important and not, and also possessed an unending repertoire of viola jokes that kept us laughing till all hours. The jokes may have been terrible, but they helped to boost our sagging egos after long days and frequently humiliating lessons. Although we may have been nothing greater than the lowest level of students at an institution staffed by legends, at least we were not dishonored *violists*. Theo, on the other hand, was significantly more reticent than Walt and was studying with a different instructor than I was. Still, he was a pianist and a year ahead of me and therefore could tell me all manner of things about my new teacher—and that was worth more to me than, well, *most* of the gossip I could get from Walt.

It was through Theo that I had the good fortune to meet a girl in the class just ahead of us, the most beautiful girl I'd ever actually seen in person up to that point. Theo had gone out with her a few times midway through my freshman year, and they remained good friends. He was, as usual, close-mouthed about their dates, but I was able to get him to introduce me to her once at a party, and I was fascinated by her charm and exotic accent. Walt had all the goods on her: she had come to the States the year before at the personal invitation of one of the faculty, who had heard her sing while he was in Europe conducting the London Philharmonic. She had been the guest artist for the performance, even though she was only sixteen at the time. With the war going on, it had taken considerable negotiation and effort on the parts of the school and the French and American embassies to arrange for her safe passage to the States. I had seen glimpses of her around and about, but even in a school that small there are hierarchies and cliques, and the voice majors and world-famous prodigies were not part of the group with whom I normally spent time. Neither were stunningly beautiful women.

Oh, that's not to say I hadn't seen gorgeous females before; I'd seen knockouts in movies many times, and downright good-lookers occasionally on the arms of other men. But Marguerite Marie Stellaire, the diminutive beauty with a voice like an angel, was the first truly gorgeous woman I had ever met in the flesh. The first one who ever spoke to *me*. I wanted everyone I knew to see Meg Stellaire hanging on *my* arm.

I knew the first time I saw her that I had to convince her she wanted to be mine.

3.5 PHILADELPHIA, 1945

MAMA

At first glance, I found Gent Jones to be a foolish adolescent who had somehow infiltrated a milieu of brilliant adults, but he was also charming and strikingly good-looking. The very first thing I noticed about him was his enchanting grin, accented on both sides by dimples so deep that to this day, I've never seen their equal. The lenses of his glasses were thick enough that through them his eyes were slightly distorted, giving him the appearance of both intelligence and mystery. Granted, I was young, but I had never before known anyone who emanated such an aura of danger and appeal at the same time. He was really quite unique in that regard.

Gent was best friends with my friend Theo, who introduced us at a party during Gent's freshman year. To put it mildly, he was atypical of the music students, most of whom were obsessed with improving their skills, practicing (my own main preoccupation), and researching and memorizing scores. Gent was more interested in improving his social standing, culturing useful relationships with everyone he met, and exploring Philadelphia. Although he seemed to have won over most of *his* class, the older students as a whole, including myself, believed he had no right to be taking up a slot at the school and that he shamelessly wasted his time. Even so, we also agreed he possessed a raw, uninhibited native talent.

Falling for him was as natural to me as cheering for the underdog.

3.6 Bumblebee, 1947

GRANDMOMMA

When Gent called to tell us he was engaged to Meg, Daddy and I had no idea how to respond.

Of course, we wanted nothing so much as for Gent to finally be happy. But it all happened so quickly, and even though I believed deep down in my heart what I had always taught my boys, that money and social status in and of themselves didn't make any one person any better or worse than the next, I also knew that he was in for a hard road. No matter what I believed, it was unlikely that Meg's remarkable family felt the same way we did. She was, after all, their baby. Beautiful. Brilliant. Talented. Cultured.

Meg had already been performing as a professional for years even before coming to the States to go to school. And much as I loved my son, he was a rough, uncultured country boy who had never had a real job or had to support himself in his whole life. How in the world was he going to be able to support a wife? And where could they fit in together? In our world? In hers? Where could they both be loved and accepted and appreciated for who they individually were?

The wedding was to be held as soon as Meg graduated, at the Catholic Church closest to the home of her U.S. sponsors in Vermont. The plan was that she would then remain based in Philadelphia for an additional year while waiting for Gent, singing anywhere she could while always returning there. She would tour the country that year as a solo artist until he was finished with school.

And then? Who knew?

But I remember how deeply Gent's daddy and I were in love when we were just about their ages. Younger, even. No one could've talked any sense into either one of us. Wild horses couldn't have torn us apart. And I've never regretted marrying him, not a day, not a minute ever since. I could only hope the same for both of them.

3.7 NASHVILLE, 2014

PROBITY

I heard Grandmomma and Granddaddy talking once about how what Gent *really* wanted was for once in his life to be a big shot, but he wasn't willing to put enough effort into it to make it happen. Before there was even time for him and Mama to get married and for him to get out of Philadelphia with his pride intact, he'd already been told he wasn't going to be allowed to return for his junior year. The problem was that if he wanted to stay with Mama, he had to stay in the same town where he got kicked out of school to begin with. It was like he was trapped there, in purgatory. That's what Grandmomma and Granddaddy said, anyway.

So there he was, stuck sweeping floors at the radio station for a year, while Mama was going to graduate with honors. It must have been awfully humiliating living in the same town where all his friends and classmates were still in school, and all the while engaged to Mama, who was already internationally known. I can only begin to guess what it must have been like for him.

He must have thought when he asked her to marry him that if she became his wife, it would build him up in other people's eyes, give him credibility. And instead, the way it turned out, it only made things worse.

If Grandmomma and Granddaddy were right, he'd wanted things to be easy, and the more they *weren't* easy, the more frustrated he must have been. Mama says as her senior year went on, she became more and more miserable thinking about traveling and performing on stage by herself, so eventually their plans for the future changed. They decided after she graduated, they'd tour together. When they could, they'd perform duets; when they couldn't, he would accompany her.

The bottom line was that she would be the star. And unlike the truth of what happened that day in the hallway with Deed, his second-class billing would be something everyone—*everyone*—would know. The fact that he wasn't quite good enough to be famous on his own was one secret he wouldn't be able to keep.

3.8 MEMPHIS, 1947

THE HOOK-UP

It's funny what you remember, and what you don't. It was summer in the Deep South. I remember that part even though I don't remember the year for sure anymore. I think it was in 1947, or maybe '48, when I first met Gent Jones. I remember he was out of school for the summer, visiting his parents who lived not far from Nashville while his fiancée was off visiting her parents in Europe. I was in a bar down on lower Broadway in Music City—I don't remember the name anymore, but it might have been "Mom's" long before everyone started calling it "Tootsie's," and *that* was long before it became her "Orchid Lounge." I was drinking my sorrows away when I first saw him across the room.

It wasn't like it is now, you know, when there are places you can go where you know you'll meet like-minded folks. Back sixty years ago or more, no one was out of the closet—not even Liberace, and he was a flaming queen if I *ever* saw one. We all feared not just for our reputations, but for our lives. There was no internet, no gay underground. There was nothing but bigotry and fear and hatred—even of ourselves.

So when you met someone, you had to either get to know them for enough years that you thought they might be safe to approach, or you had to be pretty damn drunk to make a move.

That night? I was so out of my mind you could've mopped the floor with my hair.

I could see Gent across the room, glancing at me, looking away, his eyes flickering back. I knew the move, because I'd done it enough times myself. Wanting to say something to someone, wanting to make a move, but terrified, paralyzed with the fear of what could happen if you spoke the wrong way to the wrong man. But sometimes, you know, you sink so low there's nowhere further down you can go. So you leap. And sometimes, if you're lucky, you find a soft place to land. That night was one of those times for me.

After I went back to Memphis, he came to see me a few times. He'd leave Nashville on the NC&StL train *City of Memphis* at 2:40 in the afternoon, arriving in Memphis in time for me to meet the train at 7:40. We'd have dinner and a few hours to spend together. The next morning, he had to be back at the station by 8:05 so he could be home by noon. Twelve hours and twenty-five minutes. Twelve and a half hours in which I didn't have to live a lie. Twelve and a half hours in which I could be myself.

I still don't know what he told his folks about where he was going all those nights, or what they thought he was doing while he was gone. I just know when that summer was over, he went back to Philadelphia. But all the way up until his death, whenever he was in town I'd hear from him again.

CHAPTER FOUR

The Company

"The Old Man"
↓
MKUltra
↓
Project Monarch
↓
Martin
↓
Subproject Chrysalis
↓

Field Operations	*Research & Development*	*Quality Control*
↓	↓	↓
Jäger	Teufel	Fleischer
↓	↓	↓
Charlie Osgood	Teufel's Team	↓
↓	↓	↓
Gent Jones	Luke Armleuchter	Leo Niadh

4.1 PHILADELPHIA, 1948

THE RECRUITER

I remember it as though it was yesterday. Gent Jones was still living in Philadelphia at the time and had recently been dismissed from school for not performing up to his potential. While he was waiting for his fiancée to graduate, he was working part time as the "floor manager" of the local radio station where I was to be a guest on the afternoon talk show. Floor manager was just a fancy name for janitor and gofer.

Jones was getting ready to go to lunch that day when his manager got my call. "Gent, we've got a guest for the afternoon talk show who needs a ride from the airport. Could you go pick him up? His plane was late getting in, so we don't have time to wait for a cab. He's got to be here by 1:00."

Jones glanced at the clock. 12:08. He could make it there and back. Barely. "Sure, I've got it covered," he replied. "What's his name? And which gate?"

Jones loved the chance to talk to the guests almost as much as he loved to get out of the station. It was hard for a country boy like him to live in a city like Philadelphia, and he relished every chance to do something out of doors. Running errands for the station was one of his favorite things to do.

"Charlie Osgood. Tall guy. Red hair. Gate Six. And hurry."

Grabbing the keys to the station's truck, Jones headed for the door. "What's he going to be interviewed about?" he called out just before he got out of earshot.

"Civil defense," was the reply.

Jones' heart thundered in his chest. Too young for one war, 4F for the next, he had been infected with a fear of Communism along with the rest of the country and was overwhelmed by his own fear of the Russians. Civil defense! It might not have been making a living as a concert pianist, but still it was a job he could have been proud of, instead of being stuck sweeping floors in a stupid old radio station. What kind of a difference could he make doing that? There were heroes in Si's unit; some of them he'd even known personally when he was still in elementary school and his brother had first signed up. But for him, there had been no option, no outlet, no way to make a difference. The only fighting he had done was for a scholarship and a place at a school that no longer wanted him. The only enemies he'd fought were his own laziness and the clock.

All those things raced through his mind as he sprinted to the car. Civil defense! If only there was something *he* could do to make a difference.

On the way back to the station, he asked me tentatively, "What can ordinary people do that really matters? What could *I* do that would be more important than what I am doing now? I'm smart. I can learn. I can't see well enough to enlist, but other than that, I'm in good health. Please. There has to be *something* I can do."

I eyed the eager young man cautiously. By that time, I'd had a lot of practice at sizing men up. It had gotten to the point that I could do it quickly, and I was rarely wrong. I could tell the kind of man who could be led down a path to do things he might otherwise not. I could almost smell the secrets that could be used to motivate, the potential for blackmail, if need be. This young man was eager—too eager. And I could tell that Jones' eagerness was his weakness. Eagerness could be used to get him in too deep, too quickly, before he realized he had lost all chance to back out. *Yes*, I thought. *He might be someone we could use.*

"Tell me about yourself, Gent. Tell me whatever you think is most important, in the time between now and when we get to the station."

So he did. He told me everything he could cram into ten minutes. About his talented fiancée and aging parents. About the small town where he'd grown up. And he inadvertently revealed just how desperately he wanted to do something that would make him important. He wanted to be famous. That was all it took. In just those few minutes, he showed me a weakness I could use.

As we approached the station, I handed him my card. "Tell you what, son. After you get back home, give me a call. I'll see what we can do."

Then I got out of the car, leaving Jones delightedly caressing the card. It was a plain white card with nothing more than my name, field, and phone number on it, but anyone could see that having the card in his hands made Jones feel ten feet tall. He could put it in his wallet, show it to people. I didn't know if he would ever call the number. Just having the card of someone he thought important was enough for now, and he had a way to get in touch with me if he ever decided to.

The card said only, "Charles Osgood, Civil Defense." What the card *didn't* say was that I reported to someone who reported to someone else, who reported to a man none of us ever called by name. Occasionally, the individual filling the position would change, but our name for our boss always remained the same; he was always The Old Man at the pinnacle of the CIA.

4.2 BURLINGTON, 1948

GRANDMOMMA

Before Gent's wedding, Daddy and I had never really traveled much outside of Tennessee. We went to see Niagara Falls on our honeymoon, a gift from our two families. Back then, it was just about the most popular honeymoon spot there was—whether the bride and groom *wanted* to go there, or not. But other than that we'd never really gone very far. Just a couple of trips here and there. We went to that concert when Gent was fifteen. We'd been to Memphis a few times over the years, and to New Orleans once. Not much to speak of for an entire lifetime together. Truth is, I guess it was mostly my fault, 'cause ever since we got back from the Falls, all I ever wanted was to stay close to home.

When Daddy and I started out together, we didn't have any extra money to travel. That was part of it. Who could think about going anywhere when there was hardly enough to feed the children? But another part was that I just never wanted to go anywhere. As long as I was home with the man I loved, I was happy. No need to go out looking for happiness elsewhere when you've already got your heart's desire. Ever since Daddy and I met each other, we've always been content.

Don't think it's ever been that way with Gent, though. He's never been content where he was, always looking to find somewhere else where his problems were not. The pot of gold at the end of the rainbow. Easy pickings. That's what he wanted. Awful thing to say about your own flesh and blood, I reckon, but the truth just is what it is. Easy rewards were what he was always after.

When Meg said she would marry him, he seemed to have hit the jackpot.

Her parents were furious, and understandably so. They tried to talk her out of it. They sent her older sister over here from France to try to stop it. I think, though I'm not sure, that they even tried to buy Gent off. But they had no luck. Those kids sure were stuck on each other, or at least they looked to be.

So Daddy and I headed up to Vermont state for the wedding. It was practically a second honeymoon for us, and we were by that time old married folks. The family throwing the reception said the location was their "summer home," but neither one of us had ever seen anything like it. We'd never even dreamed of such a setup.

I worried that all that finery would only make Gent more discontent with his life, instead of helping him be satisfied with what he's got—a beautiful, talented wife who loves him. I reckon I never will understand how he could ever want for more.

4.3 BURLINGTON, 1948

Mama

Up until the moment Gent and I said "I do," our wedding day was the happiest day of my life. Everyone—everything—looked beautiful. I had been to the Cathedral of the Immaculate Conception several times before, while I was spending the holidays in Vermont with my American sponsors, and every time I had found it both comforting and inspiring. On that day, though, it was especially magnificent. The sanctuary was filled with white roses; the scents of the blossoms and incense filled the air. And although politically Wagner was looked on with disfavor in those days, the wind ensemble still played from *Lohengrin*; though instead of the selection most frequently chosen, the "Bridal Chorus" which Queen Victoria selected for her daughter Princess Victoria Adelaide Mary Louise, they played *my* favorite—the magnificent Lucien Cailliet arrangement of *"Processione di Elsa nella cattedrale"*—as I came down the aisle. The priest was kind enough to do the homily in both English and French. My parents came and brought with them five of my younger brothers and sisters, and my older sister Leenie stood up for me. I knew she and my parents were having a hard time letting their little girl go, but no one said anything to ruin the day. Gent looked dashing, and had his older brother Si by his side. Walt and Theo served as ushers. The food promised to be wonderful.

Everything was perfect. Or at least I thought so.

But during the thirty minutes between leaving the church and arriving at the reception, Gent's whole demeanor changed. Before we said our vows, I was everything he ever wanted. Yet somehow, as soon as we had committed ourselves to each other, it was as though I had suddenly become a piece of property he had acquired. I don't know how to describe it exactly, but with those few words I was no longer who he wanted. I became who he had. From that day on, I never felt he wanted me as a woman again. At one point during the afternoon he spoke to me quite cruelly, and I realized that perhaps my sister was right. Perhaps I *had* made a mistake. I realized in that moment, in just the span of a heartbeat, that I had no idea just exactly who Contingency Jones really was.

There was not a chance in the world that I was going to admit it to anyone. I'd made my own bed, and I was stuck in it.

4.4 NASHVILLE, 2014

PROBITY

After Gent and Mama got married, they started traveling the community concert circuit together, with her singing and him accompanying her. My Aunt Leenie told me that when they started performing together, then it was even more obvious than ever how much better a musician Mama was than Gent. Her career eclipsed his, leaving him feeling even worse about himself than he did before—at least, that's what Aunt Leenie said.

I can only guess what parts of his life pained him the most, but I *know* one part that made Mama feel real bad. Even though he's been dead going on forty-five years, she still talks about it now and then. Still has nightmares, too, of him coming back. Bad ones. I hate that's true for her. I do love her so.

What he did that made her feel the worst was stand in front of her when people came backstage to talk to her after she sang. He'd stand there, acting like he was protecting her from the crowd, but that wasn't what he was doing at all. He was stealing her thunder. He'd stand there and pretend all that glory was due to him.

Mama wasn't much one for talking to strangers, that's for sure. And Gent did love to talk to anyone at all. But *she* loved it, too, when people said good things to her. She needed that. She *earned* it. And he stole all her attention, all the congratulations, all the admiration she needed to survive. It was like he was bleeding her spirit dry. She did all the practicing, all the work, and then he stole all of her glory. He did it from the very beginning of their performing together. And till the day he died, he never, ever stopped.

4.5 WASHINGTON, 1949

COMPANY TRANSCRIPT

"I don't know why, Martin." Teufel, the Research and Development Head, grumbled while he turned pages. "It's still not working. And I was sure the terminal experiments would be the way to get what we need."

"Yeah, I know. I keep thinking about that, too. There must be something else that goes on in the minds of children, because it's sure not working in adults. What we really need is more complete data about how MPD is created in the minds of the children who get it. We need staff members without so damn many scruples."

"I don't see why making this work has to be this hard," Jäger from Field Operations broke in. "Hell, back in Europe you can find parents who don't think anything about castrating a boy in hopes that he'll grow up to be a soprano. So why are we having so much trouble here? Why is it that around here people will give their own lives to save their children, but no one wants to give their children's lives to save their country? What do we have to do to get unquestioning cooperation *here?*"

"Americans are different," Martin said, "always thinking about their own families, and not about the greater good—or the greater evil! Most Americans have never lost anyone they know personally to the Soviets the way each of us has. They haven't lost their sons to the Communists like you and Fleischer did. They didn't see the results of the experiments in Germany, the mountains of bodies waiting to be burned. They haven't seen their own children broken and in the grave when they knew, as parents, that they should have been the ones to die first. I don't know about you, but I know thinking about my own children is what motivates me. Most Americans don't realize how much is really at stake. Maybe the real issue should be convincing U.S. citizens how important it is to know what the Soviets are up to. What would they be willing to do then, if they *really* understood?"

"Oh, come on, Martin," Fleischer, the Director of Quality Control, sighed. "We were all there; we all know, and none of us would be eager to sacrifice one of our own kids. I've spent the last four months trying to talk my youngest boy into going to college instead of enlisting, and he'd have a better chance on the front line with lieutenant's bars than he would of surviving one of our projects intact. I sure wouldn't want one of my own broken the way I've seen some of these volunteers break."

"See, that's the problem! You don't want *your* children broken, even if it is for the good of the country. We wouldn't have this problem in China, I bet, where parents are happy to break their daughters' feet, bind them, and leave them crippled for life in order to make them more attractive. We wouldn't have this problem in *any* of the countries where girls are trained from birth for lives of prostitution, or where daughters are expendable and sons are commodities expected to support their families. Hell, the Aztecs even sacrificed *their* children to their sun god! Those of us who came from Germany didn't have this problem there, before The Company brought us here. No! This is America, land of the free and home of the brave, but no one is willing to pay the price to keep it that way."

Those around the table laughed uneasily, but Martin didn't sound like he was joking.

4.6 REMEMBERING BUMBLEBEE, 1949

GENT

Those small-town, small-minded neighbors of my parents are steeped in hypocrisy. When we went back to visit Bumblebee after the wedding, Meg was welcomed in with open arms, but I could tell that underneath their welcome of her I was if possible even more outcast than I was before. It had been bad enough growing up there surrounded by those damn duplicitous Democrats, but after just three years of living in Philadelphia, I wasn't prepared for how folks back home would respond to my taking a wife who was Catholic. Somehow they are able to justify finding her exotic as a French national and world-renowned singer, while at the same time ostracizing me because she is not like them. Damn them all, every single one of them! I realize now that behind my back, folks are criticizing not just my decision to marry a non-Baptist, but worse, my choice of someone who was not a Protestant of any flavor. I'd been gone for long enough I had forgotten just how ignorant the folks in my backwards hometown could be!

By marrying Meg, I somehow violated every one of their stupid social conventions, without meaning to or even thinking it through. But I know the truth. I am superior in every way to every single one of them.

I'll show them.

4.7 NEW YORK, 1949

AUNT LEENIE

I'm deeply concerned about my little sister, Meg. Her husband is a cruel man.

He wears that mask of his and appears to be witty and charming. But I know men like him. Behind his apparently obsequious demeanor lies a man I'm sure is inherently evil.

Meg can't see it. She is blinded by her love for him, by the romance of it all. And the more I try to open her eyes to the danger he truly is, the more it seems to widen the gap between us. I've tried to tell her what I see, but she can't hear me. She only sees his surface, the side she fell in love with.

But there's something else smoldering under there. You can see little bits of it in the look in his eyes whenever someone says or does something that annoys him. He smiles, while his words slice you to bits. And I'm sure he has the potential to hurt Meg in other ways, as well.

They have a way I've noticed in the American South of justifying any biting remark by adding a phrase at the end: "Bless his heart," or hers. You can get away with saying anything that way. "That boy is dumber than a rock, bless his heart." "She's ugly enough to stop a clock, bless her heart."

Gent makes the same sort of cruel remarks, but doesn't bother to soften or disguise them with the blessing. His words bite right through to the core.

Meg may not be able to see it now, but from the outside, I can see how he wounds her. She left France for the States a confident and competent young woman, and every time I see them together, I see him undermine that foundation a little more. The reason he can get away with it is that it's in such tiny increments she doesn't notice. His cruelty is insidious, like slow poison. Day by day, he's making her doubt her own judgment. I fear for her, the darling little sister I love.

4.8 DES MOINES, 1949

MAMA

It was late one Saturday night, and we stopped at a roadside motel. The concert had been breathtaking. Sometimes, you know, everything falls together. The piano is in tune, the interpretation is exquisite, and the acoustics of the hall match both the instrumentation and the size of the crowd. Everything is perfect.

That night was one of those.

It was the last in a series of three concerts in one week that ended the fall season. We were headed back to Gent's parents' home in Bumblebee for Christmas afterwards. We drove as far as we could, then stopped at a little motel. I was feeling quite romantic. Even the little dive where we had stopped off to eat had been decorated with lights and tinsel, and I was thinking of home. My second Christmas with Gent. I thought his parents were delightful, and my sister Leenie was going to come down from her new home in New York, bringing her new husband she met at *my* wedding and as many of my favorite baguettes as she could carry on the plane. They'd be a few days old by Christmas morning, but I knew they'd make our breakfast taste like home— even if they were so hard all we could make was French toast. It was going to be sweet. Christmas with our little family.

But when we got to the room, out of sight of the desk clerk, Gent started in on me again. I don't know why I constantly kept setting myself up for disappointment. I always imagined that things would be different, and then, when they weren't, it hurt more than if I had just expected the worst. I set myself up by hoping. It was my fault. By then, I knew better.

When he could tell I was hurt, then he told me *that* was why he didn't want me, that my skin was too thin. He said he was afraid to be around me when he was angry, said he didn't want to say anything else till he calmed down, so he was going to get a cup of coffee, and he left. He was always saying that to me. He didn't want to speak to me in anger. He was afraid he'd do something we'd both regret. He'd be back when he calmed down.

That night, over two hours went by and he still hadn't come back. Eventually, I sneaked out of the room and over to the small honky-tonk bar across the street. He hadn't taken the car, and it looked like the only thing open within walking distance.

When I entered the bar, he didn't even notice. He was dancing with a woman he had picked up somewhere in just that short time since he left. They were pressed together and were moving so suggestively I was humiliated. I watched for a moment, and when he ran his hand down her leg, I crept back to my room and cried myself to sleep. He didn't come back until dawn.

4.9 BUMBLEBEE, 1949

UNCLE SI

It broke my heart when I came home for Christmas to see what Gent is doing to that lovely girl. Being around him makes me feel crazy, because he says things and pretends to be one way, while you can tell that he's still mean as a snake underneath. It seems he has everybody else snowed. But not me. My memory is better than that.

I abhor what he's doing to Meg. She is beautiful and has talent in spades, but he puts her down every time he gets a chance. Whatever she suggests, even if it's something as unimportant as where to go for dinner, he intimidates her into doing what he wants. If she tries to enter into a conversation, he just bulldozes over her. He may not be hitting her with his fists the way he used to hit me when we were kids, but you can see on her face and in her posture that his actions are having the same effect. He's still hurting people. The difference is, now he uses words.

I've seen it before, in the army. In basic they beat you down to nothing before they build you back into the killing machine they want you to be. But she has done nothing to warrant this—nothing. And how could anyone want her to be anything other than the remarkable woman she already is?

Gent may be my brother, but I want to beat the daylights out of him when I see him treat her like that. He's not the little brother who needs protecting anymore. He's a grown man who is abusing someone less powerful, and *she* needs protecting from *him*. If I ever find out Gent is still hurting people now that he's a man—if he started physically hurting Meg or anyone else—well… I'd have to make it right somehow. I'd do whatever I had to do. I'd do what I should have done when we were kids.

CHAPTER FIVE

5.1 BUMBLEBEE, 1950

MAMA

A few months after Christmas, I found out I was pregnant. By then I was desperately lonely on the road. With only Gent for company—and our feelings for each other as diametrically opposed as they possibly could be—all the time we spent together only exacerbated my despair.

We were basically living in hotel rooms. My parents were on the other side of the ocean. My sister Leenie was by then married and settled in the States with a young one of her own on the way. All my friends from school had blossoming careers of their own. With no place that felt like home base, I found myself totally isolated and alone.

I wanted to move up north—preferably to New York, where concert possibilities beckoned. It was closer to my American sponsors in Vermont, and Leenie would have been right there, too. It would have been a comfort to be close to her when both our little ones were born.

But Gent wanted us to move back to Bumblebee, and had countless reasons why we should move there instead of further north: We couldn't afford to get a place of our own. We weren't yet seasoned enough to take New York by storm. A child would be happier growing up in a small town with grandparents nearby than in a large city. A woman should leave her family and join her husband's, and his family was in

Tennessee. Being around my sister interfered with our living our own lives. His list went on and on.

No matter what I said, he had an answer for it. My concerns were belittled, my wishes minimized and rationalized away, one by one, as all of his, one by one, won.

5.2 Bumblebee, 1950

GRANDDADDY

Gent wants to move back home. He thinks it will be economically rewarding for all four of us if our two families share household expenses, and he says he knows how desperately Mother and I want to be around the grandchildren when they come.

That's what he says.

But as always, with Gent, I wonder if he has another agenda. They spend their lives traveling; we'd be free child care. They want to live in a house with a yard; we've got one already. He's always been one to want to take the easy way. I'm worried what that means.

So Mother and I sat down and put our heads together, and came up with some rules for if we live in the same house.

Some of them are the rules we've always had, like if you make a mess you clean it up. Others are more specific to this situation—we don't mind taking care of children on the weekends, but when the law office is open and Mother and I are working, Gent and Meg are responsible for finding someone to keep watch. We're not willing to have two families crammed into this tiny house we've lived in since we moved here, but we *are* willing to sell this one and pool our resources with Gent and Meg to buy a large, rambling farmhouse that has just recently come on the market. The most important one, in my mind, is the one Mother and I agreed to between ourselves. We've decided to stick to it whether Gent and Meg agree or not.

We believe young people should work things out for themselves, and we have agreed never to interfere. Ever. If we're going to live in the same house with them, they will have to make all the decisions regarding their family for themselves, and we will not intervene in any way. We've decided we won't even give advice should we ever be asked for it. The bottom line is, that boy's got to grow up.

5.3 NASHVILLE, 2014

PROBITY

I've heard Mama tell stories about the day Ernie was born. She says it was the happiest day in her life up 'til then. In Ernie, she at last found somebody to love her completely, the way she'd always loved him from even before he was born. Somebody to need her and not say mean things to her. Somebody to always be glad to see her.

By then, Gent must've been being mean to her, too; he couldn't have maintained being nice to anyone for too long. But I guess back then nobody got divorced, especially not Catholics. And she must have known he wouldn't have let her take us back to France with her if they did. Once Ernie was born, Gent had her for life.

I know they disagreed about religion more than once in my hearing, and I bet they started arguing about it as soon as Ernie was born, maybe even before. Gent had apparently agreed before the wedding that we kids would be brought up Catholic, but since they had moved back to Bumblebee he had the perfect excuse for not doing so—Bumblebee was so small there was no Catholic presence at all, except for Mama and two German women who had married soldiers. When I was small, I used to hear Gent and Mama argue, Gent saying it couldn't be helped, and Mama saying, "But you promised." Mama always wanted to take us to the little Catholic church at the county seat. It was so tiny it looked like a dollhouse made of stone. Gent always said no. And he always won every argument.

It was funny, though. They never argued in front of us. In front of us, Gent's word was always law. It was only from behind closed doors that I ever heard Mama disagree.

Ernie was followed five years later by me, and then almost three years after that by Equity, so by the time eight years went by, Mama had three children in tow. I only ever had the one, so I can't imagine how she did it. Makes me tired just thinking about all those diapers and sleepless nights. And all that time, she was practicing her singing and performing and traveling on the road, lugging us along with her every time she could. She was—and is—amazing. I may have been mad at her more than once—at one point when I was younger, I was even mad at her for years—but I still do admire my mama so.

5.4 BUMBLEBEE, 1958

MAMA

The eight years between the births of Ernie in 1950 and Equity in 1958, with Probity born between them, were a whirlwind of concerts and chaos.

In the beginning, most of our concerts were duets in small towns; they were easy to book and kept us busy on a regular basis. Gent and I would drive in the station wagon with Ernie in the back. Well, Gent would drive, and I'd ride along. He didn't like to relinquish control even long enough to let anyone else drive the car.

Some days it was fun, riding along with Ernie, pointing out horses and cows as we drove down the highway. He was always on the lookout for cows, and would burst into a fit of giggles every time he pointed at one and I exclaimed, *"Vache sacrée! Holy cow!"*

But other times, it was exhausting trying to keep a toddler entertained and quiet in the confines of a car so that Gent wouldn't get mad about the noise.

As Ernie got older and my reputation grew here in the States, flying alone was easier and I was invited more and more often to perform at venues like the ones I'd enjoyed in Europe. I'd leave him with Gent and his parents, and would have a few glorious days to myself. Singing with symphonies, receiving warm accolades after my performance at Carnegie Hall. On those days, standing onstage alone, I didn't have to worry about whether or not Gent would be sulking backstage after the concerts, and I was able to reconnect with why I loved to sing.

But Gent didn't like to book those concerts. He didn't like my being onstage—or anywhere for that matter—without him, so I wasn't able to enjoy those experiences often. He wanted to be involved, always, and would go along with my performing solo only when it was absolutely necessary to pay the bills. Otherwise, we stayed on the small-town community concert series circuit, performing together.

With Probity's birth, Gent seemed only to get angrier. I couldn't tell whether it was that he had always wanted a son and once he had one he didn't want to be bothered with any more children, or if it was jealousy because an additional baby meant the children were taking more of my time away from him. In either event, after Probity came along, I was never able to go back out on my own again. With Equity's birth though, his icy heart seemed to thaw. After two children who looked like me, Equity, at last, was a child who looked like him. Perhaps it was just easier for him to love a child who reminded him of himself. After her birth, he seemed genuinely to want the children to travel with us, instead of merely to tolerate it. Then, for a while, things were better.

5.5 BUMBLEBEE, 1958

GRANDMOMMA

Oh, my goodness, that precious little Probity reminds me so much of my beloved Deed. When she was just starting to stand up and walk on her own, she would smile when she was walking towards me just like he did. They were both such beautiful babies, towheaded, blue eyes, and their smiles—goodness, *gracious*, those two children looked just like each other. Deed hadn't yet stopped looking pretty as a girl before he died, with his long lashes, curly hair, and fair skin. He always looked at me with complete and utter trust and adoration, and giggles—golly, I loved the way he laughed before his life got cut short. My heart still aches for that child, God knows, but Probity, looking and laughing so much like him, well, she does help to fill that gaping wound.

Lord, I thought it would never happen, but someday, with this one, maybe I'll finally stop hurting so badly and start to heal. Stop waking up in the night grieving, wondering what could have been. She puts her scrawny little arms around me, and I can just feel his through hers. Poor little Deed never even had enough time to grow into a tumbleweed of a boy like his brothers.

I remember all about tumbleweeds from growing up in Texas where everything that wasn't tied down blew with the wind, tumbling through the desert with nothing to stop it but the occasional cactus. All three of my boys were always like that, nonstop movement, covered with a thin layer of dirt within minutes of getting out of the tub. Their hands, their faces, their feet—anything they wore attracted dirt like a magnet. Probity's just like Earnest that way, too; all of them always into one thing or another.

Not like the baby, I can already tell. Equity's not that way at all yet, and you can tell she's not going to be, ever. Even though she's barely sitting up, she doesn't like for there to be a speck of dirt on her. Dark like her daddy, but delicate, she is, and beautiful, too. We'll be having to beat the boys off that one with a stick.

5.6 WASHINGTON, 1958

COMPANY TRANSCRIPT

"All right then," Martin said. "Let's go over it again. Teufel, run it through for us one more time from the beginning. We know others have gotten it to work. There has to be *something* we are missing."

"I don't see how there can be. We've tried manipulation, coercion, extortion, drugs, sleep deprivation, torture, terror, termination. I can't imagine what's left. There is nothing we can find that guarantees a subject's personality will split. Nothing. All we know is that sometimes it does."

"No, Teufel, I mean really from the beginning. What do we know, what do we need, and what stands in our way?"

"There's no point in this, Martin. We've been over it so many times I can do it in my sleep. It doesn't do any good to keep going over it, over and over again. We're not getting anywhere."

"Okay then, just give me the short version. One more time."

"You're the boss." Teufel sighed as Martin closed his eyes and leaned back in his chair. "From the beginning. We know for a fact that fracturing the mind is possible in kids. We also know that so far we haven't been able to cause a single case of split personality in any willing adult volunteer. Unfortunately, our research into how it is, exactly, that this process works in kids has been hampered by the fact that we have also learned that their minds are more likely to split the smarter they are. That means that the populations we've had easy access to, whether poor and desperate enough to sell a kid for drugs or money, or unknown, unloved, and unlikely to be missed if kidnapped, have not provided us with subjects intelligent enough to be successful.

"We know we need kids who are off-the-charts smart, but it's not practical to steal subjects from brilliant parents, because in America those parents would be more likely to come looking for them. We've learned that it is hard to find staff who are willing to work with kids who have been bred and grown specifically for the purpose—inevitably one staff person or another's ethics gets in the way. Too many scruples here about damaging 'innocents'. And we've learned that it is difficult—not necessarily impossible, but difficult—to encourage the staff we do have to carry out experiments with subjects to their logical conclusion, if it means causing the kind of trauma we believe we need in order for these experiments to be successful. So that takes us back to adults, and in adults, it doesn't work."

Martin leaned forward and slowly opened his eyes, looking at each face in order around the room. "Okay. We've been working on this project, from one direction or another, for ten years. *Ten years*. For ten years we've been unsuccessful at causing multiple personalities in adults. We would like to do more research with children to see exactly how it is that MPD is created in them, but we've eliminated buying or breeding the kind of children we need. And we've disqualified most of the staff. But damnit folks, I know this stuff works. We've got documented cases of multiple personalities in adults. We're pretty sure all those cases were developed subsequent to brutality, rape, torture and/or murder, but we know they exist. We didn't make this up. We know those cases are out there. And we didn't have to create them—their parents and caretakers did. This is *not* a new idea. Surely there is some way to replicate these results in adults. And I'm sure I don't need to remind you that your jobs depend on your figuring out how."

5.7 NASHVILLE, 2014

PROBITY

Back in the '50s Nashville was just beginning to spread out, and Bumblebee, being nearby, was growing like a weed. I guess they must have been scrambling to find enough volunteers to do all the things even a small town needed to have done. Since Gent was always trying to get folks to like him, or even better, to look up to him, I guess that's why he volunteered to chair the Civil Defense Committee. Every once in a while, he'd even show off this worn and shabby old civil defense card he carried in his wallet, like the name on it was supposed to impress people, but it sure didn't mean anything to me.

Whenever he and Mama were in town, instead of practicing with Mama like she needed him to, he spent all of his time encouraging all our friends and neighbors to prepare for nuclear war. He preached the importance of storing up on supplies of food and water, and teaching all of us children to duck-and-cover in case any bombs fell nearby.

Our own house was stocked like a fortress for a siege. The basement was bomb-proofed, with mattresses around the walls to protect against nuclear fallout. Cases of canned vegetables and big metal cans of water were stored there, along with a freezer stocked with half a cow; my suspicion now is that Gent hadn't spent quite enough time considering the possibility of being stuck in the basement with a freezer full of rotting meat if and when the power went out in the event of a nuclear war. Everything was rotated up and through the kitchen in the house above and then replenished in the basement on a regular schedule, just like the war-preparedness materials said.

While Gent was running around trying to be a big shot, Mama was left at home trying to hold everything together. I can't think that Gent was ever much actual help to her. In front of other folks he was always bragging about how much work he did to take care of us, both at home and on the road, but that wasn't the way I remember it. Seems to me, he was always badgering Mama to keep us quiet or to make us behave. Just to cover his bases, he'd beat us when she couldn't make us meet his standards. But he always made a point out of telling us he'd never hit us in anger. He'd wait 'til his blood ran cold. Then he'd tell us it hurt him worse than it hurt us.

I never did believe him, though. Never.

5.8 BUMBLEBEE, 1958

GENT

People on the road ask us all the time why we carry the kids with us everywhere we go. Actually, we don't take them *everywhere*. But we do take them everywhere we can.

After Equity was born, we bought an old, used school bus and converted it into bunks and a bathroom, so now when we have to drive anywhere we can pile the kids in there with all their stuff. Meg teaches them their lessons while I drive. They want for nothing in our care.

My parents didn't always correct my bad habits when they presented themselves and I've always wished they had made me a better man. I'm not making the same mistake with my own. If *my* children are dishonest, or disrespectful, or lazy, I am right there to put an end to it on the spot.

There is nothing more important to me than being a full-time father. And people get that, too. I tell everyone my motto is, "Whip your children every day. If you don't know the reason why, they do." When I say that, people laugh, and I think most of them think I'm kidding. I'm not.

I don't quote scripture much, but this one I know: Proverbs 13:24 says, "He that spareth his rod hateth his son: but he that loveth him chasteneth him betimes."

I don't hate my children, and I don't want anyone thinking I do.

5.9 BUMBLEBEE, 1958

MAMA

Gent puts on a big show, but what it's really like carrying the kids with us is not what he'd have everyone believe.

He makes like we're a big happy family, but our life is not always what it seems. There is never any doubt that at every minute Gent is in control. He controls where we go, when we leave, why we stop, what we eat. If the children make too much noise, just because they are children, he expects me to keep them quiet. And if I don't, he beats them. Just the threat of that makes me physically ill.

Unsurprisingly, he doesn't call it "beating." He usually calls it "spanking." But they were still in nappies when he switched from spanking them with his hand to whipping them with a yardstick—one of the big, thick ones he gets at the local lumberyard, with the lumberyard's advertising running down the backside of the stick. And he beats the children's uncovered backsides with them.

When we're at home in Bumblebee, I try to go outside or upstairs while he spanks them, or somewhere else where I cannot hear the children cry. He says it is for their own good, but I don't know. I don't think so, but no matter what I say, he always has some reason from some psychology book that says I'm wrong. He may be right, but I can't bear to hear it.

On the road, though, there is nowhere I can go to get away from their cries, and because there is nowhere for them to go outside to play, it gets worse day by day. I hate living like this. I hate him. And because I can't figure out any way to make it any better, I even hate myself.

5.10 WASHINGTON, 1958

COMPANY TRANSCRIPT

"Maybe that's it!" Teufel smacked his hand on the table hard enough that the coffee cups rattled in their saucers. "Maybe the trick is *not* to start out trying to replicate the results in adults. Since we haven't been able to figure out how to do that using children we can get to on the sly, then maybe the trick is to coerce parents into 'volunteering' their children for our research. Maybe we could get greater cooperation if somehow we set it up so that the parents thought *they* were in control. I don't know if mothers would do it, but fathers might. And everybody has a weakness, if only we can find it."

"Yeah. I see where you're going with this," Fleischer said. "If we started out by blackmailing the parents, we'd be able to access the kids more freely, and wouldn't have to worry about what they said when they went home. We would have greater leeway to do whatever is needed. Maybe then we'd figure out how it was done."

"Hmmm. Has possibility." Martin thought about it, running his fingers through what was left of his hair. "Every case of split personality we've looked at seemed to have been caused by one or both of the *parents* torturing or abusing the child. Getting the parents involved. I wonder if that's part of it? I wonder if, for the personality to fracture in the precise way we need it to, if it needs to be *parental* torture. Maybe it causes greater trauma if it's someone the child is attached to who's the betrayer. It's an angle we haven't pursued before."

"Actually, I wasn't even thinking that, but it could be. I was thinking that perhaps parents could be coerced into 'volunteering' their kids if they were allowed the illusion that they were retaining control. What you're saying takes it a step further. Maybe, if we could convince parents that there would be something in it for them…?"

"Okay then, Teufel. Your team's in charge of that. In order for it to work, we'd need a structure that a parent or parents could follow, and we'd need parents who would benefit in a substantial way from their children's participation. Or at least, they would have to *think* they benefited. Somehow they'd have to be 'encouraged' to keep quiet. It would have to be something no one would talk about, that no one would admit to, or if they did, that no one would believe.

"Jäger, you put the word out in the field. Quietly. We need parents who want something—anything—as long as they want it badly enough. Parents of really smart children, so more than likely the parents need to be above-average intelligence, as well. Professionals, probably. People with something to lose if they are found out. And people with something to gain if they're not. What we need to save America," Martin went on, "is a group of parents willing to violate everything Americans hold sacred."

CHAPTER SIX

6.1 BUMBLEBEE, 1958

ERNIE

Bless him. *Bless* him. *Bless him.*

They told us that verse in Vacation Bible School one morning, the one 'bout doing something nice for people who are mean to you 'cause when you do, you heap burning coals upon their heads. So I keep praying God'll bless Papa *every night.*

I don't like it when he give us spankings, but I can take 'em. Not like Probity. She's such a baby. She's always making a big deal out of *everything.*

She always cries when Papa whips us, but not me. I'm almost eight years old, and I can take *anything.*

She says it's not fair, an' she didn't do anything wrong. Or she says she doesn't know what she did. But that's only 'cause she's stupid and doesn't know what's *what!*

I do. We're bad an' we deserve it. She doesn't know what's what yet 'cause she's only three. And she's a *girl.*

We get spanked two times every day, after breakfast just before I go to school, an' after supper before we go to bed, 'cause we know what we did. Except for *Equity.*

Equity doesn't hardly ever get whipped. She doesn't do anything yet 'cept eat an' sleep an' cry. She can't even stand up an' walk. She's a *baby.*

It's no big deal to get a whipping, 'cause when we're bad, we deserve it. We know what we *did*.

When I get to be a man someday, I'm going to let my children do whatever they want so they never deserve a spanking an' nobody has to hit them *ever*.

6.2 BUMBLEBEE, 1959

Mama

Gent and I may be taking in quite a bit of money on the front end, but the expenses of keeping up a concert career must be enormous. It seems no matter how many concerts we book, we barely break even. Gent thinks we'll do better if only one of us is in charge of keeping up with the accounts, so he's in charge of the money. But as he explains it, all the money is absorbed by plane fares and hotel rooms and gas for the bus, or else it's sucked up into our share of the expenses of keeping up the house.

To help make ends meet, he recently wrangled a part-time job as a writer for one of the Nashville daily papers. Since he writes feature articles about what we're doing on the road, he can do it no matter where we are. That way, he doesn't have to be away from me or the children often, though it would certainly make our lives more pleasant if he did. Sometimes he's gone, but not much.

That helps some, but not enough to take the pressure off of him. He keeps blaming the psychology books he reads all the time for his paranoia. He says he believes sometimes people are watching him. And I can't figure out how to make it any better.

The best I can do is to make sure he feels in control of the things he *can* control, because when he feels in control he seems calmer. It's so bad that at this point, he controls virtually every aspect of our lives together. He's become so obsessed with controlling everything that, as the man and the head of the household, he even puts the food on our plates and fixes our drinks, and no matter what it is or in what quantity, the children are forced to eat it before they can leave the table. That's especially hard on Probity because she almost always feels sick when she eats. Her reluctance to go ahead and finish her meals and get her spanking over with only makes his temper worse.

He is determined that if lack of self-discipline on his part was the result of his own parents' permissiveness, then he is not going to repeat their mistake. His "discipline" results in his punishing the children harshly and often, frequently for no reason at all that I can see. In many cases, he doesn't even bother to give a reason they are being punished, because they are supposed to "already know." He may not have the discipline to take control of his *own* life, but he is determined that he will not be an excuse they can use later for the same. Occasionally, he demands from them a confession for some real or imagined transgression, and if no one dares confess, then he beats them all and tells them it is the fault of the guilty one that the other two are being punished.

No matter what it is, it's never *his* fault, not even his inability to finish the novel he started long ago about the war, *All's Fair*. He says it's a love story about a soldier who sacrificed the possibility of marrying the one he loved in order to marry a foreigner who provided him the cover he needed to spy in another country. Even in his fantasy, he's the hero whose unhappiness is someone else's fault. In his book, as in our lives, he blames the main character's unhappiness on the foreign wife. He's been working on it for years, but like most of his goals, it still remains unfinished.

COMPANY TRANSCRIPT

"He's a concert pianist, for heaven's sake! His wife is a singer! Gent Jones and his wife travel all the time. We can use that to our advantage."

"I'm not convinced, Martin." The Old Man paused for a moment and considered. "Say we do decide to make use of him. How do we know we can trust him? He is totally undisciplined. I don't have any reason to believe he wouldn't attempt to use us for whatever purpose suited him. This is *not* a real spy we're talking about here. Jones is nothing more than a man who pretends to be whatever he thinks will work to his advantage at the time."

"Jäger's man Osgood's been keeping tabs on him for quite a while now, Sir. Unlike some of these men, who led relatively clean lives up till we sucked them in, Jones has a lot to hide. He's been leading a double life at least since he left home for college, and maybe before. We've traced him to a number of sexual relationships with women and with men—relationships all over the United States, some of which have lasted for years. We know he has an innate predisposition for cruelty. It has been suggested that he may have murdered his younger brother—whether by accident or on purpose, we don't know. We have evidence of significant long-term violence and sexual perversion. And it's all hidden behind his demure concert-pianist persona. He has a *lot* at stake if his secrets ever get out. I really think we can use him."

"From you, Martin, that's saying a lot." The Old Man laughed. "You don't trust anybody!"

"Oh, I didn't say I trusted him. But I think we can use him. And I think we can blackmail him if necessary. I'd like to suggest that we do.

"He has a built-in cover for traveling widely, even internationally, if need be. He has a gift for interacting with all types of people, from the highbrows who come to hear his wife sing to the lugs who set up his piano. Simply by having our assets attend a few concerts, the community of concert musicians, artists, and supporters could provide the perfect cover for communicating our directives around the different projects. He and his wife already return to some towns year after year, so it would be easy to work them in wherever we needed him to be. They even take those children with them almost everywhere they travel. No one would suspect him, Sir. No one."

6.4 Bumblebee, 1959

Mama

Sometimes I wish he'd just go ahead and hit me and get it over with. There is always the silent threat hanging over my head that he wants to. Maybe if he'd go ahead and do it, he'd finally feel better and I wouldn't have to keep being afraid he will.

I don't know what else I can do to make him happy. There's nothing I can do to change the fact that I'm the main draw when we perform together, which infuriates him more and more each day. He already controls everything tangible—the contracts, the bank accounts, the bills. Everything goes through him. I receive top billing, but I only get to spend what he decides I should have.

He's the one who took that extra job. I didn't ask him to. And no matter what he says, he took it because he loves to write. He thrives on the attention. But now he holds that job over me as though it was the greatest sacrifice of all time. He doesn't think that my caring for three children and practicing every day so that we can maintain a successful concert career together should count as two jobs for me, too. He certainly isn't putting in the hours at the piano that he should be. When you add in trying constantly to keep him from exploding, it seems to me my job count ought to be three.

6.5 BUMBLEBEE, 1959

THE RECRUITER

One cold December morning, I was waiting for Jones when he arrived at the small diner he frequented for breakfast in Bumblebee's county seat. He was obviously surprised to recognize a familiar face from his college days. "Charlie? Charlie Osgood, is that you?"

A purposeful grin spread across my face. "Gent Jones? Is that really you? What are you doing here?

"That's some memory you've got for names and faces!" Jones exclaimed. "I live here. What are *you* doing here?"

"At this moment, I'm just sitting here waiting on a couple of over-easy eggs, toast, bacon, and coffee, but the reason I'm in town is to do the same old boring thing I do all the time, traveling the country checking out local Civil Defense committees." I paused a moment, then grinned again. "Do you have any idea who's in charge of civil defense around here?"

"I *do* just happen to know that, Charlie; *I* am! I teach war-preparedness classes all over the county, talk to children in schools, set a good example by what we do at home. I'm doing what I can for the country." He sighed. "I've never given up hoping for something more glamorous, though. The closest I've come is trying to write a book about a war hero, since I can't be one myself."

Over breakfast, we swapped stories and small talk, as each of us imagined what the other's life was like. My practiced eye took in Jones' disappointment and discouragement, and a weariness that had crept in where once he was so eager. "Tell me about your family," I asked, so he did.

"My oldest child is so smart that ever since he started school, he's been at the very top of his class. The one in the middle hasn't started school yet, but she's even smarter. And the youngest," Jones smiled so widely dimples took over the cheeks on either side, "is the apple of her father's eye. My wife is still beautiful, too, in case you're interested."

"Of course I am," I laughed. "It's important what kind of an impression the civil defense representative makes in the community. Front line personnel can ultimately affect national security as much as the President's staff."

"Don't tease me, Charlie." Jones' demeanor fell abruptly. "You know how I felt about making a difference ten years ago? Well, I still do, and you see what I'm doing. Don't make fun of me." Jones fell silent, and for a moment, I did, too.

"Come on, Gent." I slapped a bill down on the counter and got up from my stool. "I've got your breakfast. Let's go for a walk."

Outside, it was one of those cold, cloudy winter days, dry but not looking like it would stay that way long. The dreary sky reflected the discouragement that had taken over Jones' mood. Few cars were out. It was too early for the shops around the square to be open, but we headed in that direction, anyway.

Downtown was only nine blocks altogether, three squared. The four-story courthouse stood smack dab in the center, its dome taller than any of the surrounding buildings except for the seven-story building that rose above the bank across the street. On the opposite side of the square, a single building housed the city hall, the community center, the police station, the library, and the fire department. Shops ran down the other two sides. Other than the "skyscraper," it was virtually identical in every way to every other small town in the South.

Together, Jones and I sat on one of the wooden benches underneath the magnolias surrounding the square. Jones slowly ran his hands over the scooped-out hollows on the bench that had been carved away over the years by old men and boys sitting there waiting for their wives and mothers to shop, with pocketknives in their pockets and nothing else to whittle on other than the bench itself. He stared at the top floor of the building over the bank as he did so; I watched him.

"What would you be willing to do to really make a difference?" I asked quietly. "What would you *really* be willing to give up?"

"Anything," Jones answered. "Absolutely anything at all."

THE STREETWALKER

I thought I'd seen it all.

You know how it is on the streets. There's all kinds of men out there, and it's not always the good men who hire the likes of me. Sometimes it is. The quiet ones, the gentle ones, the ones who are too shy to ever ask the target of their dreams for a date.

But there are cruel men out there, too, and sometimes we get them.

Last night, for instance. This guy was walking down the street I was working—I had a great corner, too. It's usually not a bad job. Pick up some badly needed cash. The work's frequently disgusting, but not hard. If you ever need to make some extra money, I could give you some pointers, if you want. But that guy last night? Men like him make you want to reconsider going hungry and being cold instead.

You could tell he wasn't from around here. Sometimes they talk, you know, and you get an idea where they're from. This guy started out calling me "Sugar" in a voice just dripping with honey. He sounded like a good-old Southern boy right up till he got me in the alley. Could've been acting, but I don't think so. Wherever he's from, I hope he goes back there and stays.

He wasn't just cruel, he was vicious. Brutal. Evil. The sex was violent. Humiliating. Degrading. Like he hated me, and I have no idea why.

Sandy found me later, beaten unconscious in the alley just around the corner, and wanted to take me to the hospital, call the cops. But what could I say to them? Arrest me, please, and take me in because jail is safer than the streets? The guy was no one I'd ever seen around here before, a stranger who's probably left town already.

God, I hope so. He was a creep, even if he did call himself a gent.

6.7 NASHVILLE, 2014

PROBITY

I haven't always called him Gent, you know. I didn't start doing that 'til after he died. I reckon he would've beaten me for being so disrespectful if I'd done it while he was alive.

During all those years I couldn't remember anything at all, I always referred to him as "my father," but then when I started remembering, I always called him by his name after that.

But before that, when Ernie and Equity and I were small, I always called him Papa. It was Papa, I remember now, who was sometimes nice to us.

My favorite thing he would do was read us the bedtime stories. He didn't come in each of our rooms and read us some little kid's story like they do in some people's houses. At our house, we all climbed in Mama's and Papa's bed and he got out some grownup novel and read us one chapter a night. Every once in a while he'd read us two. Papa would do all the voices himself. We loved that part.

Sometimes, if we'd been good and it was early enough, he'd even read us something short at the end, like an encore after a concert. *Uncle Remus* was the best. I 'specially liked his voices for Brer Rabbit and the Fox. "*Please* don't throw me in that briar patch" was the very best line.

It wasn't all bad, you know, growing up with Gent. Just most of it.

6.8 Bumblebee, 1959

GRANDMOMMA

Si came home for Christmas on leave, and told me a story. He started out saying something had happened when he and Gent were kids, and it was all his fault. But then, he never finished that one.

Instead, he told me about something else that happened recently overseas. His platoon was supposed to be moving civilians away from the boundary of the base, and they had found a place with a spring where they thought the villagers would be safe. They loaded the families and their belongings into trucks and delivered them to the site, which was about an hour's walk away. A week or so later, the soldiers woke up to discover that overnight the villagers had started coming back.

Si said he was furious. They were working hard to keep the locals safe, and their thoughtfulness was being rejected. He woke the translator and stormed out the gates of the compound to confront them, demanding to know why they had returned.

The water was bad there, one father said, so they came back 'cause their children were dying. They had a little boy, just about two, who was one of the dead. Si said the boy had reminded him of Deed.

And then he fell apart. All I could do was hold him while he wept. He never did go back and finish telling me about what must have been the day Deed died.

6.9 NASHVILLE, 2014

PROBITY

I'd like to think Gent struggled with the decision, but I don't suppose he did so for long. Brother hadn't been born yet then, so he only had three of us children to choose from, after all, and only one of us was a boy. I'm sure he didn't want it to be Ernie, his firstborn and only son. And the truth is that he wouldn't have wanted it to be my little sister, either. Parents weren't supposed to have favorites, but Equity was his, and we all knew it. That left just me, the one in the middle. Now that I'm older, I can see why I would've had to have been the one. If it was me, then, if anything happened, that would still leave him with a daughter and a son.

Of the three of us, I was not only the one who was most expendable, I was also the smartest. Not to brag, but it was true. Might not have had much common sense, then or now, but I read faster, learned quicker, remembered longer. I'm sure he'd have thought that'd make them happy, too. They'd have probably told him they wanted smart, since what I hear now is that worked best. And at the time I was just turning four, so that would've been to his advantage, too. He still had more than a year before I started school, a full year in which he still had control of me twenty-four hours a day. *Yep,* I'm sure he thought to himself. *It'll have to be Probity.*

And now that I'm thinking about it, I was probably the easiest one for him to get away with abusing, too. There's a running joke in our family about there not being a single picture of me as a child smiling. Unless I was with Grandmomma or Granddaddy, or Mama's parents Gran and Gramps were in the States, the only thing I ever really did was read. I was already way too serious for my own good. And I didn't talk much, either, at least compared with the other two. If the experiments affected me badly, who'd ever know the difference?

Yeah. I guess I had to be the one. That way, no one would ever have to know. The one he would give them would be me.

CHAPTER SEVEN

7.1 BALTIMORE, 1960

COMPANY TRANSCRIPT

"Okay, what have we got?" Teufel looked around the table at the research and development team, studying each face in turn. Five men sat quietly, studiously looking back at him, no one eager to go first. The table had chairs for seven, but one of their number was running late. Tardiness was frowned on, so it didn't happen often. No one spoke.

"No volunteers? Then Johnson, you go first."

The thin man toyed nervously with his glasses. "So far, we have sixty-five potential candidates. We'd like to narrow those numbers down to thirty-six, since our target is three solid groups of twelve. We believe any group of more than a dozen is dangerous. Too many chances for things to go wrong. Too much likelihood someone will talk. Four of the candidates live in towns where we are likely to be successful, and each of those towns has a potential politician we might be able to draw into the mix, too. That would give us a little extra cover in case we need any help with the local police. Each of the candidates lives within a day's drive of at least one of the four towns."

Teufel nodded, and Johnson visibly relaxed. "Williams?"

"We've checked out all the kids. All sixty-five have IQs of at least 140. Forty-six have ages ranging from six years old to nine. Eight are between three and five. Eleven are between ten and twelve. Every one of the fifty-three already in school is way ahead. From what we can tell, not a single one of them has ever experienced a major prior trauma. Ideal subjects."

"Sounds good. Graves, what do we know about the parents?"

Graves stirred nervously in his seat. "Every subject has at least one parent who is at home most of the time. Unfortunately, most of them are mothers. We've had a hard time coming up with enough professional fathers who can keep their kids on a leash. But we've got a dozen so far, writers and actors and musicians, mostly. We're likely to have an easier time getting compliance from them than with the women."

Teufel frowned. "A *dozen?* You know better than that. Our goal was that *all* of the children would be accessed through the men."

"Oh, we've got access," Graves stammered. "We just don't have constant supervision."

"That's too dangerous." Teufel's voice darkened noticeably. "Mothers can't be counted on. Women are too soft for serious experimentation, especially where their own progeny are concerned." The color began to rise in his face. Around the table, grown men froze.

"We'll keep working on it. But if you're determined that all the subjects have male handlers, then our potential prospects at this point are down to twelve."

There was an explosion of anger. "You've had months to get this list together! Would someone like to explain your failure, as a group, to follow orders?"

This time, it was the quiet man at the other end of the table who spoke up, representing Jaeger's team. "It's asking a lot, you know, to find professional men who work from home and have access to their kids round the clock. When you throw into the mix that they also have to have kids who are downright brilliant, that narrows the number even more. But to find men willing to do what we're asking? It's virtually impossible. We've been working day and night, Teufel. We can find men who are mean enough to do what we want. We can find men who are smart enough and have smart kids. We can even find men who keep odd hours and work from home. But finding just the right combination of all these in a man we can control? All I can tell you is, we have twelve. Each of them lives within a day's driving distance of one of three towns. Five live within distance of one, four of another, and three of the last. If you're telling us we're *only* working with men, then we're down to three test sites. One is in the South. One is in the Northeast. The last is in the Midwest. Twelve subjects. Three sites. That criterion effectively makes the decision for us. We don't have to go any further." He spoke with finality. No one moved.

7.2 BUMBLEBEE, 1960

GENT

There's something about Probity that brings out the worst in me. Anytime she doesn't do what I tell her to, I want to hit her.

Keeping myself under control is important, but less so than getting her ready, and there isn't much more time before we begin. By then, she needs to be totally compliant. I expect her to be the best.

She's too young to understand this is all about national security. I'm not doing this just to be mean to her, so I explain it every time, in words I think she'll understand. "I would never hit you in anger. This is for your own good. It hurts me more than it hurts you." Even as smart as she is, she's too young to understand that there is much more at stake here than her feelings. It is *her* country I'm trying to protect, too.

I keep reminding myself that there's still a little time. They've given us a schedule to keep, but I want her to be one step ahead of everyone else when it starts. This is not an ordinary contest because the stakes are the world.

I plan on being the one who wins.

❖❖ 7.3 BALTIMORE, 1960 ❖❖

COMPANY TRANSCRIPT

Teufel glared at the end of the table, but did not look directly at the speaker. Finally, without acknowledging what had been said, he went on. "Abrams?"

"We have a mole ready to plant in each group. Our guy will be the contact. And since we can't risk losing our only witness in case of an 'accident,' there will be a second plant in each group as well, as a control. The moles don't know about the second plant. The second will report directly to Fleischer."

"Have you got them picked out yet?"

"Fleischer selected them, and he won't even tell *us* who they are. We'll probably be able to figure it out, though, in groups that small..."

"What did you end up with for the composition of the groups?"

"Our goal has always been a dozen adults in each group with the kids. We originally thought all those adults would be their parents, but since it looks like we're going to be running this project with fewer subjects than we originally planned, we'll fill in the rest with, as much as possible, politicians, law enforcement, anyone we think we can blackmail or use. As much as possible, we're planning on throwing in a few women, to keep the balance. We'd rather not use the mothers if we don't have to, though a couple seem to be eager to participate. If we can't find other women who are suitable, we'll throw a few hookers in the mix."

Teufel nodded, then frowned. "Where's Haas? Anyone know why he's late?"

"Don't know, Boss, but we can brief you on what we've got." Abrams took a deep breath. "In theory, the group will be set up with meetings following the lunar calendar. That will get them together at least monthly on full moons. Each of the kids' birthdays will be 'celebrated' one of those times. We had figured twelve to a group would come out to about one birthday a month, but since it looks like the number of subjects will be smaller, we'll throw in a couple of other holidays, as well." He paused, looking at Teufel, who didn't say a word.

"In the beginning," Abrams continued, "we'll start with something small—just enough to convince the kids to keep quiet. Over at the naval base we found that killing small animals in front of them works pretty well, so we'll probably go with that. The trick is to suck the parents in, to get them to be complicit in what's happening, so more than likely we'll go pretty quickly from the first phase to the second."

❖❖ 7.4 BUMBLEBEE, 1960 ❖❖

GENT

It's going to be really easy. I don't even have to recruit the group members—Charlie's already given me a list.

I'm in control of making the contacts, finding a site, setting it up, and running the meetings. I know just the place. They've even given me something to make Meg sleep through the whole thing.

The whole process is choreographed, like an elaborate play or lengthy ballet. The fun part for me, where I'll really get to use my thespian skills, will be the extemporaneous part. The Company can't control all the variables, so it will be up to me, the one with my boots on the ground, to improvise, essentially serving as emcee. I'll be the one to keep things moving, roll with the punches, keep us to the timetable. They're worried about us going too fast, moving the subjects through the process before they have achieved maximum conformity. That part's up to me, too. I have to keep the group under control, while letting them think *they* have control.

This is the perfect job for me. It uses all my skill sets—my positive experiences with practicing something till it's perfect; my ability to stage, act in, and direct a drama; my excellent interpersonal dynamics; my innate skills with kids. Charlie and his buddies don't have any idea how much I'm going to personally enjoy enlarging my sexual repertoire and number of partners, and I'm not going to tell them. No way I'd give them the satisfaction of knowing that.

They even gave me a cookbook-style set of instructions on what works best to keep the subjects from telling. It's going to be easy. A little drama, a little torture, a little sleight of hand, a little truth. This role was created for me. I'll be able to bake their cakes.

The only issue I have with the current format is that they insist whoever offers the sacrifice each time— whether it is me or someone I have chosen—has to wear a robe and a mask. I'll do it, because they said anonymity works best; when the subjects can't be sure who it is, they'll learn it could be anybody. They'll learn not to trust anyone. They'll learn there's no one safe to tell. But I resent their feeble attempts at control. The sacrifice is clearly going to be the highlight of the ceremony. I want everyone to see me in my moments of glory. I want them to know *it is I who wields the knife.*

Within *my* hands lies the power of life and death.

7.5 ATLANTA, 1960

THE MOLE

When Jones first contacted me, I'd been waiting. He doesn't have any idea yet that I am a plant, a mole put into play to report everything he does to The Company.

I had no idea it could give me such a thrill to watch him go through his spiel, to see him struggle to look natural, like he'd done this thing or something like it many times before. You could tell he's been reading those spy novels by Ian Fleming, because everything he did or said was a caricature of the main character. You could almost see him thinking it through: *What would James Bond do?*

What a joke! *My* family really *is* what he wants to be, so I know a pretender when I see one. I don't have to think about how to respond. I *am* of noble blood. What *he* is, is the village idiot.

The Company has suggested I nurture a friendship with Jones and his wife, Meg. What a looker! That part should be easy. Like taking candy from a baby. Or in the Joneses' case, their innocence.

So, in a few weeks the wife and I are going up to Nashville to go with them to dinner and the symphony, and soon they'll come down here and we'll do the same again in Atlanta. They want me to keep up the façade as long as the project lasts. I can do that.

He really has no idea who I am or what I'm really here for, and that gives me power over him. He thinks he's in control, but he never truly will be. He'll only have as much power as I decide.

7.6 BUMBLEBEE, 1960

GRANDDADDY

Something in this household doesn't feel right lately.

Mother and I are worried about the grandchildren, but we can't put our finger on what the problem is. Even if we could figure it out, we aren't sure how to address it. In the beginning, when we all decided to live in the same house, we made the decision to stay out of Meg and Gent's business. But at this point, whatever is going on has us troubled so deeply we're wondering if we should make an exception.

He's brought home some new friends lately we don't approve of. He's started to drink way too much. His temper gets worse all the time.

Listen to me! I sound like I'm talking about a teenager. Well, in the meantime, we made an agreement to stay out of it, so we're sticking to it for now. Gent and Meg need to be the ones to work this out. Our intervening won't make a man out of him. I don't know if anything can.

7.7 DETROIT, 1960

THE CONTROL

Ah, what a tangled web The Company doth weave. Armleuchter is firmly entrenched as the mole in the Tennessee project, but then Fleischer's got me as a control watching both of them.

When they told me Jones was our Bumblebee asset, I was thrilled. I had actually met him and his wife before. The first time I saw them was when he and Meg were on the road, performing in Detroit.

I fell in love with her the moment I saw her, and that was before she had even begun to sing. With her first notes, I was enslaved. I've traveled many times to hear her since. Once I even flew across the country to hear her in San Francisco on a weekend I had no other plans. Several times, I've gone backstage to try to talk to her, but Jones fiercely guards the gate. Every time, though, it's been worth it, even if all I can say is, "Thanks, it was wonderful."

I can't decide if that is going to make this assignment more painful or more enjoyable, but whichever it is, it will certainly make it more complicated.

❖❖ 7.8 BUMBLEBEE, 1960 ❖❖

PROBITY, AGE FOUR

One night a week, we get to watch TV. Papa makes popcorn an' fixes soft drinks with ice we grind up with the grinder that hangs in the kitchen, an' once we're all seated, he passes them all 'round. We get to watch for three hours. *Three hours.* First, we watch the news. Then we mostly watch westerns like *The Rifleman* or *Bonanza* or *Gunsmoke.* But sometimes, we get to watch things like *Ed Sullivan*, too. It depends on what night of the week it is.

Mama can't ever stay awake long enough to watch the shows all the way though, but I can. She falls asleep 'bout halfway through her popcorn an' drink, an' Papa has to pick her up an' carry her to bed.

Then, after everythin' is quiet an' ever'body else is asleep, bad things happen. I try to hide between the mattress an' the wall where the monsters can't find me, an' I watch the light of the nightlight in the doorway hoping they'll stay away. But when the shadows come across the door, bad things are comin'. I'm pretty sure there are monsters in my closet, that in the daylight I can't see.

When the board creaks in the floor outside my door, I can't breathe. I close my eyes an' pretend to be asleep. It doesn't do any good. The monsters always come an' find me. Most nights they climb into my bed an' I can't hide. Sometimes they pick me up an' carry me away.

❖❖ 7.9 Bumblebee, 1961 ❖❖

Gent

Right from the beginning, our instructions were easy to follow. Before we'd start, we'd tie the subjects up where they could see what we were doing, hanging them upside-down from tree limbs by one foot. The directions Charlie gave me set out everything we were to do, step by step. Even the chanting and movements were all prescribed for us, but the sex we ad-libbed. It was too good to put into words. I'd never experienced anything so exhilarating, not since those first early days in Interlochen. There's always something special about your first that you never forget.

The first one you finally give yourself to. The first one who gave in to you. The first one you hit. The first one you raped. The first one whose life you took with your bare hands.

First times are the best. Each time, you think it is the greatest thrill you've ever experienced. Each time, you wonder how to top it, when you'll ever feel that fully alive again. By my age, you wonder what's left.

At first the subjects would close their eyes and cry, but it turned out to be pretty easy to make them watch. We rarely had to use anything other than verbal threats to pets or family members, but I wasn't above using physical violence when necessary. It was for their own good, after all... well, theirs and the good of our country. Didn't take much practice to become an expert at controlling my punches so I could hit them hard enough to cause significant pain, while pulling the punch just as contact was made to make sure the blows rarely left a bruise.

I got better at it every time.

7.10 NASHVILLE, 1961

PROBITY, AGE FIVE

Grandmomma an' Granddaddy are Southern Baptists
and they say they brought Papa and Uncle Si up that
way, too, but the only time Papa will ever let us go to
church with 'em is for the one week in the summer they
have Vacation Bible School. For VBS week, every kid in
town gets to be a Southern Baptist.

Each day for a *whole week*, a different one of us is
chosen to carry the Bible up to the front in the parade,
an' another one reads out of it, an' today, 'cause I'm
five, I got to be the reader. It was *really* scary sittin' up
on the stage in one of the big throne chairs waitin' 'til it
was my turn to read. I was afraid I'd do it wrong. Or at
the wrong time. Or I'd make a mistake readin' an' then
somebody would be mad at me, even though they
promised when we were done we'd get grape Kool-Aid
and peanut butter crackers for snacks. We never *ever*
have that at home.

The verse I read today was really confusin'. I mean,
I know what evil is, an' bein' bad. I understand what
cruelty is, like bein' mean. But that verse I read today
from Mark was 'bout bein' nice. It said somethin' like,
"an' Jesus, lookin' on him, loved him." I've thought
'bout that all day, 'cause the man it was talkin' 'bout
hadn't done what he was s'posed to have done. Jesus
wanted him to do somethin' different, but nobody hit
him, nobody said he knew what he had done. It just
said Jesus looked at him an' loved him an' then told

him what he ought to do instead. I still feel confused when I think 'bout it. Papa says he hits us 'cause he loves us an' that all the bad things are for my own good. So does or doesn't that man Jesus love me? He sure sounds nice, though.

I never have understood why Papa won't let us go to church any other time. He says it's 'cause he doesn't believe any of that stuff an' he doesn't want anyone else tryin' to convince us of it before we are all grown up an' can make up our own minds for our own selves. That's what he says. Most of the time, though, I just think he doesn't want us to go 'cause they are nice, and he's bein' mean.

CHAPTER EIGHT

COMPANY TRANSCRIPT

"I wish Haas were here with his chart to show you," Abrams said, "but phase two focuses on the adults first having sex with each other in front of the kids, then with animals, and then actually involving the kids. Should traumatize the kids thoroughly, and get the adults in deep enough that they can't get out."

The man at the end of the table spoke again. "Chances are that if we can continue phase two long enough, these guys—at least at this point, it sounds like we're in agreement that all the parents will be guys—will get to where they're starting to get off on the power they will wield over the kids. I've heard that most of our rapists enjoy their work whenever the excitement equals or exceeds the fear of getting caught. The longer these men go without getting caught, the more likely they are to enjoy the activities. Then, the thrills will have to keep getting bigger to give them the same rush. We're not sure how long phase two will last, but when they start beginning to push the limits, it will be our signal to move on to phase three."

❖❖ 8.2 Bumblebee, 1962 ❖❖

Gent

The move from intercourse with the other adult group members to experimentation with animals is coming soon, so I've been checking with the other groups to see if they are ready, too. The Company wants all of us to keep to the same timetable so their results will be accurate and comparable. Sex with the subjects will be coming up soon after that.

I keep reporting regularly to Charlie. The buzz I get from having the fate of the country in my hands is almost unbearably orgasmic at times. When they threw me out of school, they had no idea who they were messing with. This month, with all the news about the missile crisis in Cuba, I see every day how important this job is. I am finally going to be a hero. Si will never know, unless I tell him, that I'm finally bigger and better and more important than he will ever be.

I'll have to decide whether it's worth it to tell him, or if it's more delicious to keep it a secret.

When we started the project up, they gave us a schedule of actions to take to ensure the subjects never tell. Some assignments they gave us are things we are supposed to do every single meeting to program them to self-destruct rather than tell anyone else what goes on. Most of those have to do with making sure they think someone is watching them all the time and that if they tell we'll know, and that what we would do to them then would be worse than if they killed themselves.

Then there is some new action assigned for every month, and all of those are arranged to be consecutively more traumatizing. We started by killing the subjects' favorite pets in front of them to make sure they knew if they told, that would happen to them, too, and then we escalated from there. Now that we're getting ready to move up to the next level, they've had us ramp it up quite a bit. With Halloween coming in a couple of days, they had us borrow a coffin from one of our more esteemed members, complete with a corpse that's about to be buried. It's handy having a mortician on board.

We'll be digging a hole and we'll take turns burying each subject in the casket with the body. They don't have to stay in there long—Charlie's instructions told us exactly how long to leave each subject underground. I'll have to try to remember their responses, since I won't be able to write anything down till I get home. If the subjects had any question about our intentions before, they won't after this.

After Halloween, they'll know we are serious beyond the shadow of a doubt.

8.3 DETROIT, 1962

THE CONTROL

Everything is moving right along. We've got one of the group members in Bumblebee running for state senate, so we're right on target. The Company says they will make sure he's elected, so that part's not my concern now. My job at this point is simply to shepherd the legislation through when the time comes, so I'm laying the groundwork now. In Colorado, we've already begun. We're starting with just the dozen states where the kids who are our current subjects live, but our goal is to make it nationwide.

The excuse of lobbying with state legislators has made a great cover for traveling across the U.S. It's also made it possible for me to orchestrate dinner with Jones and Meg a couple of times already. That part is a long-time dream come true.

The part I hate is what's happening to the children. I understand the psychology behind it. I understand the importance of being able to develop separate spy personalities in adults. But I hate, I absolutely hate, that we are using children to research how to do it. I've even heard some talk that if we are successful with the children but not with the adults, we'll keep tabs on these children throughout their lives so we can continue to use them as adults, if need be. It'll take longer that way, but in the long run it may be our only hope. There's a separate programming protocol going on attempting to connect any separating personalities with certain sequences of code words that should be effective no matter how many years in the future.

I may not have children of my own, but that doesn't stop me from finding it distasteful to be a part of abusing these. It is especially difficult for me with Probity, who looks so much like her mother. I try to stay away from her on the nights of the meetings. Though I'd like to, it would be too obvious to avoid them all.

8.4 HUNTSVILLE, 1962

THE TRAVELER

We had no idea what to expect. It was such an honor to have one of our children chosen, even though neither of us was thrilled by the protocol when they told us about it, and we sure weren't looking forward to the drive, which was going to take three hours each way.

Then, when we got up to Bumblebee the first time, we discovered that there are other families participating from out of state as well. None of us want the drive to negatively effect the results because the kids are cranky and wound up when we get there after being in the car so long. We all want them to have the best experience possible, and to do our part for the country. Even though none of us live all that close to Florida, given all the news lately about Cuba, all the kids are still practicing duck-and-cover. We all want them to be able to do even more.

So last time, all the out-of-towners agreed that from now on, we'd come early. Everyone is bringing something for a potluck—I've had deviled eggs and potato salad in the cooler all the way, trying to keep the kids and the hubby out of there so there'd still be something left for everyone else to eat when we get there. Another of the families said they'd stop and pick up bar-b-que and baked beans when they drove through Nashville so it would still be hot when everyone got to Bumblebee. Someone else is bringing dessert and drinks. We should have quite a feast!

This will work so much better. This way the kids can unwind from being in the car, play in the churchyard, and run around and get some of that energy out! After the sun goes down, the last of the locals is going to come bringing his daughter. And once everyone has arrived, then we'll begin.

❖❖   8.5 ATLANTA, 1962 ❖❖

THE MOLE

I'm constantly aroused thinking about the next ritual. Sex with children, all of them virgins, prepubescent girls and boys, incipient whores, and all of it sanctioned by the United States government. It is simply too perfect.

Thinking about it, anticipating it, has made it impossible for me to contain myself at home, and I have finally shown my wife what she should expect from now on when she doesn't listen. Last week she went out for groceries and spent more than she is allowed, and I'd had enough.

I've hit her a few times before, but this time I let myself go. So much more satisfying to beat her within an inch of her life. She lay on the floor, sobbing hysterically, while I forced myself into her ugly, bloody body. I didn't even notice her eyes were black and her arm was broken until I got up.

It wasn't as satisfying as I anticipate the kids will be, but it was a start.

❖❖ 8.6 BUMBLEBEE, 1962 ❖❖

PROBITY, AGE SIX

I can't breathe. I'm crushed between 'em. Papa an' the bad man are hurtin' me. *It hurts.*

PLEASE STOP! IT HURTS!

I'LL BE GOOD, I PROMISE!

I promise, next time I'll be good.

Please hurry.

Please hurry.

Please hurry.

Please hurry please hurry please hurry I can't breathe.

I promise I'll be good.

COMPANY TRANSCRIPT

Graves spoke up. "The third phase is where we're likely to run into the most resistance, so it will be important to have the parents thoroughly entrenched before it begins."

"Phase three," Abrams picked up, "will be when we enter into the terminal experiences. If we don't have multiplicity before then, that's when we expect the kids to break. At that point, we'll start using the programming sequences to try to trigger personality changes independently of the trauma. And if we can make that happen, then we'll finally have what we've been looking for: the ultimate, the perfect spy."

Teufel looked at the ceiling, pursed his lips and looked back at his team. "To be accurate," he said grimly, "we'll have a handful of mentally enhanced minor subjects who, if we're lucky, we may be able to activate later to become spies. But it would be a start. It's more than we've got now."

❖❖ 8.8 BUMBLEBEE, 1963 ❖❖

GENT

No matter what we did, we just couldn't get Probity to break. They'd been having some luck with a couple of the subjects in the group out in Colorado, and I sure didn't want anyone else to succeed before I did. I was starting to feel desperate.

By then we'd been at it for almost two years, and each month she got quieter and more withdrawn until she finally reached the point that she hardly showed any emotion at all. She had almost quit talking altogether, even when we weren't in the woods, and she never laughed aloud anymore—not even that murmuring sound she'd made before, the one that was so quiet it was almost like a dove cooing. I hadn't heard her make that sound in months. But even after she got to the point that she didn't bother to cry anymore, we just couldn't get her to split. The whole thing was becoming exceedingly frustrating.

Finally, Charlie brought a suggestion from the team developing the protocol. On the Halloween night after Probity's seventh birthday, they supplied us with the sacrifice we were to use. God knows where they got it—probably "adopted" from that home for unwed mothers in Nashville, or flown down from some late-term abortionist in New York, or bought from some mother who needed drugs more than another mouth to feed. By then, I'd learned never to ask.

I thought the timing was perfect, though—Meg was always whining about the fact that Probity was past the age when she should have received her first communion, and hadn't. She was seven, after all. But I had an even better rite of passage in mind.

That night, it seemed like the ritual dragged on and on. I just knew that night was going to be the one. That was going to be the day we achieved multiplicity. That was going to be the night when everything paid off.

When the time came, I carried Probity up to the altar. She knew what was coming—she had to know—yet she did not resist in any way. She didn't try to stop it from happening, or fight against me. She did just what she was supposed to, as though she knew it was her destiny to do so as surely as I knew it was mine. I wrapped my hands around hers, holding her tiny fingers firmly around the knife.

And together we plunged the blade through the whimpering infant's heart.

CHAPTER NINE

9.1 BUMBLEBEE, 1966

PROBITY, AGE TEN

It sure is embarrassin' being so much younger an' lit'ler than ever'body else in my class. Bein' smart hasn't ever done me much good, either.

Bein' smart doesn't do you any good when you start school when you're five an' they test you an' then they test you again an' then they move you to the third grade and ever'body there already knows what's going on but no one bothers to 'splain it to you 'cause they think you're smart, an' you overheard 'em saying you didn't really belong there either, but it was the best they could do.

Bein' smart doesn't help when you wanted to be in the Girl Scouts but it would be too embarrassin' to be the only Brownie in the third grade so you don't even ask, so you don't find out 'til years later that if you *had* asked you might've found out it doesn't work that way, an' not ever'body has to start as a Brownie no matter what grade they're in.

Bein' smart isn't doing you any favors when you read in a book how to play solitaire, but the book doesn't tell you that you can't win every game, so you spend the first couple of years you play feelin' stupider an' worse 'bout yourself every time you lose, 'cause you can't figure out how to make it work.

Bein' smart only makes you feel worse when you get a spankin' 'cause it hurts, an' then you have to add onto that how bad it makes you feel 'bout yourself 'cause he tells you that you ought to know what you did, but you can't figure it out.

Bein' smart doesn't mean you know any more than anybody else, it just means you take tests better, so you're stuck bein' two years ahead of ever'body else in your class. An' that means two years littler. I sure wish I wasn't.

People thinkin' you're smart means you're always waitin' for the day somebody finally figures out you're not an' then they'll put you back where you belong, an' that'll be even more embarrassin' than bein' where you are. I know what that's like, 'cause I'm always afraid it'll happen to me.

I shouldn't really even be in the seventh grade. I'm only ten.

I've been thinkin' 'bout that all day today 'cause when Ernie and I got on the bus this mornin'—it was goin' to be my first day in junior high—I was so little the bus driver asked me if I was sure that was where I was s'posed to be.

It was so embarrassin' I couldn't say anythin', so Ernie had to 'splain it to the bus driver for me.

When I got to a seat, the rest of the way to school I kept wonderin'. He was askin' if I belonged on the bus. That's not what I want to know. The real question for me is, do I belong *anywhere?*

9.2 BUMBLEBEE, 1966

GRANDMOMMA

I'm so worried about that child. Ernie's not doing well either, but at least he's older and he seems more at home in his own skin. Even so, I'm just sure Gent beats that boy when we're not home.

He treats Equity like a little princess, and she seems oblivious to whatever's going on. But Probity. For some reason there's something else going on there, and Daddy and I don't know what.

We keep trying to figure out what to do, but we're afraid if we intervene he'll cut us off from those babies completely. We've seen him cut other people off before. We don't want to be next.

Daddy and I may not know what to do now, but Gent could make it so we wouldn't be able to do *anything* later, even if we figure it out. We're still living in one house, and if Gent and Meg move out, or we do, we wouldn't be able to keep tabs on what's going on at all. At this point, it's a risk we're not willing to take.

If it doesn't get any better, maybe I'll talk to Si about it. He was always able to control Gent pretty well when they were kids. He might be able to figure out what's going on. And he doesn't have as much at stake since he doesn't live at home with us anymore. Maybe Gent will listen to him.

9.3 NEW YORK, 1966

AUNT LEENIE

Gent's meaner to Probity than he is to either of the other two. And I'm not just making it up—our parents have commented on it every time they've come over from France. I have no idea why. I've been telling Meg for years: there's something not right there. And this week she finally confided in me that she's afraid.

She's afraid of Gent. She's afraid for anyone to find out. She's been ashamed for me to find out I was right about Gent all along.

She's right, I admit it. I'd have given her a hard time about it, said *I told you so*, probably for years. But ashamed! In front of me, her own sister! I never wanted that.

I wish I had known. I don't know now what I could have done differently, but I do know I would have tried. If I had realized my behavior made her feel that bad, I'd have made every effort to change.

We're here alone in the States, after all, Meg and I. It is only the two of us, with no family here except for each other. But I know—I *know*—that together we can face anything. I love my sister completely. She may not believe it, but there are many people who would do whatever they could for her. I know, because I'm one of them.

Meg may not have much self-confidence left, but she deserves to have it in boatloads. I've admired her from the very first time she stepped out onstage alone. She stood there like the little thing that she was, in front of that huge audience filling the hall, as though she had belonged there since the beginning of time. No one would have ever guessed she was afraid that night, too, but I remember that she was. She overcame her fear then to win over the world, and I know she can do whatever it takes even now.

She was such a young thing when she left home to come to the States, young and beautiful and brave. More courageous than I'll ever be, I tell you. And from the moment Gent met her, he has done everything he could to extinguish her beauty and undermine the courage within her.

9.4 BUMBLEBEE, 1966

PROBITY, AGE TEN

Papa was on the road this week. I like it when he's gone. Then it's just Mama, an' Ernie, an' Equity, an' me at home with Grandmomma an' Granddaddy. I like it that way.

Ernie's always bossin' me 'round whenever Papa's gone, like he thinks he's the daddy or somethin'. But I sort of like it, 'cause it makes me feel special.

He's leavin' for college at the end of this school year, an' I hate that. I pretend I'm glad an' I won't miss him, but really, I will.

When Papa got back home last night from wherever it was that he went, he found out Mama let me spend the night with my new best friend from junior high. I never spent the night at anybody else's house before. I never really even *had* a best friend before.

Mama was happy for me, but Papa wasn't. He was furious.

It was the first time I *ever* saw him get that mad. I don't even know what he was so mad *for*. It wasn't like I did anythin' I wasn't s'posed to. Not that I know of, anyhow.

But instead of bein' mad at *me* this time, he was mad at *Mama*. He was so mad he didn't even have on his I'd-never-hit-you-in-anger face. I *never* saw him that mad before.

He was screamin' an' his face was all red an' twisted up, and he kept screamin' at her over and over, "If you can't control her," (he was talkin' 'bout me), "I will."

THE TRAVELER

That bitch! That whore!

We've been bringing our kids out here to these woods for *years* now trying to change history and she is undermining all our hard work!

They brought her in tonight to entertain the men, brought her in blindfolded, from God-knows-where. And look at her!

Instead of waiting her turn quietly like she's supposed to, she's over there comforting the children, undermining everything we've done! I *saw* her! I *heard* her! She's stroking that little girl in the cage, telling her it isn't her fault! Telling her everything's going to be okay!

You should never have brought her here! She'll ruin everything!

I don't *care* if you blindfolded her. I don't care *where* you got her!

She might figure it out! She might tell!

She can *still* entertain you. *She* can be the sacrifice!

Kill her! *Kill* her! *Kill her!*

❖❖ 9.6 BUMBLEBEE, 1967 ❖❖

GENT

Tonight was the most profound experience I've ever had.

It was one of the women's idea, actually, which is troublesome because it really should have been my idea instead of coming from one of the members of the group. Though it wasn't on the timetable Charlie gave me for any of the upcoming meetings, the sacrifice of an unsuspecting human adult—someone old enough to know and appreciate what is coming—is the next logical step in the progression of trauma-producing stimuli we are applying to the subjects.

It was exhilarating. No one was expecting it, from the whore to the subjects to the members of the group. Till that moment, neither was I. That was what made it such a powerful experience, I think.

That's what they have me for: to respond, right there on the spot, to the dynamics of the group, to improvise whenever it's called for. It would have been obvious to them if they had been there last night that what was called for was sacrificing the whore.

The group's energy visibly increased as the out-of-towner incited them. It was educational just to sit back and observe. She was able to project her own fears and paranoia onto the group so that theirs increased exponentially. Eventually, all of them had the same heightened emotional and physiological responses she had, and all of their responses increased over time.

It was truly fascinating to watch. Once I realized what was happening, it was easy enough to step back in and regain leadership of the group. I simply had to make them think that what they wanted had been my plan all along. Child's play.

It was the sheriff's deputy's turn to kill the goat, so I let that go ahead as planned. He poured the blood over the whore as she lay there, spread-eagled on the altar, legs and arms tied open for the orgy. Then, when all expected the orgy, instead, the *coup de grâce*. Oh, God, it was exhilarating.

When I stepped up to segue from one act to the next, I picked up the mask and the robe from where he'd laid them. I pulled the mask over my head, put the robe on, and picked up the knife. Having seen it happen once to the goat, she realized what was coming, and it was at that point she began to scream. It was exquisite. I started the chants, and the group realized, too. Their cries, their dancing became even more frenzied, building, building, until I cut out the whore's heart, right there where she lay.

She was expecting an orgy; they all were. And it was an orgy, all right. An orgy of sensuality, of emotion, of power!

It was the most exhilarating experience I've ever had in my life.

❖❖ 9.7 BUMBLEBEE, 1967 ❖❖

PROBITY, AGE ELEVEN

We were drivin' along in the car when Papa stopped to talk to the old man. He was dark, like Papa's friend Billy, but where Billy is young an' strong, this man was all wobbly an' old, an' he had to sit down on the curb while Papa was talking to him.

Then it got really confusin'. Papa says we're s'posed to treat ever'body the same, just like Grandmomma says. But then, he didn't do it. He started treatin' that old man real mean, an' callin' him that name we're not s'posed to call anybody, *ever*—the one he beat me for when I came home an' said it after I heard it at school, before Grandmomma 'splained that it wasn't a nice word to use 'cause it made Negroes feel bad 'bout who they were. But nobody had ever told me that before, or I wouldn't have. Papa could've told me first, before he hit me, like Jesus did with that man in the story I read from Mark.

When the old man wouldn't get in the car like Papa told him to, Papa started hittin' him in the head and grabbed him up an' shoved him in the backseat with me. I was s'posed to be asleep, but I was cryin', an' Papa wouldn't stop.

An' then we drove to where the bad things happen.

THE RECRUITER

"Good God, Gent! What are you doing? Have you totally lost your mind?"

"Take it easy, Charlie. You'd have been proud of me. I was doing just what you chose me for, facilitating the leadership of the group."

"There was nothing about what you've done recently that has been officially sanctioned! Nothing! You could completely throw off the results of the whole project by not following the protocol exactly. What in the world possessed you?"

"It was easy, Charlie. I took care of everything. You don't have to worry about a thing."

"What do you mean, I don't have to worry? The first one, you're telling me was an impulse, but the second you planned? You *planned* to completely disregard direct orders?" Charlie shook with anger.

"The first one, the 'impulse' as you put it, was just a whore we had hired for the night. We picked her up off the streets in Nashville, just off of Dickerson Road. There are hundreds of whores in that town, Charlie. No one will miss her.

"The second, the old colored man, was even easier. He was falling-down drunk, walking along on the road towards home. I know for a fact that he's got no family, no friends to speak of. No one will come looking for him. It was safe, Charlie, I swear it. All I had to do was look around to make sure no one was within eyesight and offer him a ride. He climbed right on in, passed out in the backseat till we got to the site. He never knew what was coming until it was too late."

"I appreciate your attempt at taking care, Gent, but you *cannot* keep this up! I have to take it to the team. I have no choice. I have to see if there is any way they can mitigate the damage you may have done to the protocol. Your impulsive decisions could ruin the entire project."

"Oh, come on, Charlie. You know we'd have gotten there eventually, anyway. What's the real issue?"

"The real issue? The *real* issue? You're out of control! You have to stick to the protocol you've been given and you cannot 'pick up' people so close to home. You're from a *very* small town. Someone will notice if the crime rate goes up. Someone, somewhere, will come looking."

"But I can't just stop now. We're building to a crescendo, and I can't expect them to go back to something less exciting. What do you propose I do in the meantime?"

"Oh, God, I don't know. You've put me in a terrible position. Let there be no question about my feelings about this: You *have* to stop selecting your own sacrifices. You have to leave that up to the team.

"If you seriously cannot control your own impulses between now and when we come up with a plan, then for God's sake, Gent, at least pick up someone farther from home. Get a hitchhiker, for God's sake, from the interstate, at least a couple of hours away from Nashville. Don't choose *anyone else* you know or who can be connected in any way with you or the program. And don't make any other changes to the protocol until I've had a chance to run all this by the team.

"Don't push me on this, Gent. Don't forget what we know about you. We know about your peccadilloes, your sexual aberration, your violence, and now your murders. You toe the line on this issue or we'll make sure everyone else knows about them, too."

9.9 BUMBLEBEE, 1968

MAMA

Tonight I was too tired to watch television with Gent and the kids, so I just went straight to bed. Gent didn't want me to, but I've had the flu, brought on by exhaustion after battling the measles with all three kids in a row. I can't keep anything down, not even liquids. Didn't think I could sit up with the children to watch even one show through to the end, so I just went to bed.

When I heard something, I awoke. I thought everyone else was asleep until I heard footsteps and the floorboard that creaks in the hallway outside the children's rooms. I went to nudge Gent to ask him to check on them, but he wasn't there. When I got up to check myself, I saw his back, at the end of the hallway. He was headed down the steps.

And he was carrying Probity in his arms. I know it was Probity because Equity's hair is dark like his, and the blond hair on his shoulder was too long to have been Ernie's. He was creeping along so silently I was afraid to make a sound. I wasn't sure what was happening, but something wasn't right. I was paralyzed by fear. I didn't want him to know I had seen.

Maybe Leenie is right. Maybe something really is going on. I don't know what, but whatever it is, I don't like it. It doesn't feel right.

I'm too sick to figure it out tonight, but now I know. If it happens again, I will follow.

❖❖ 9.10 Bumblebee, 1968 ❖❖

Probity, Age Twelve

That cute little boy was jus' playin'.

Papa told us to be quiet, an' I *told* that little boy he'd better listen to what Papa said. But he didn't.

He didn't listen, so Papa picked him up an' smashed his head into the rock. I sure wish he hadn't. I couldn't protect that little boy. It was all my fault, 'cause I couldn't figure out how to stop it. I feel terrible.

I'm always the most afraid before the killin'. You never know who it will be. Sometimes, like tonight, it's someone out of the circle. I never know when it'll be my turn, so when the mask an' the robe come, that's when I'm always the most afraid.

After the killin' part's over, I'm not so scared. I don't like the next part, but it's not as scary as the killin'. Unless they pass me to the bad man. He always hurts us the worst.

First there were five of us kids who came every time, an' now there are only four. That means all the grown-ups will get more turns. Even the bad man.

If I'm not good enough, I'll be next.

I'll be next.

I'll be next.

CHAPTER TEN

10.1 ATLANTA, 1968

THE MOLE

This is child's play, planting these little seeds of discontent among the group.

Jones is always the last one here, kissing Meg's pretty ass, making sure she's drugged and down for the count before he leaves home. He's making this so easy for me it's hardly any fun. No challenge. The group is putty in my hands until he gets here. Another few months, and I'll have them all eating out of my hand.

Just a little, "I'm worried someone will find out," in one ear. "He's going to get us caught," in another. Or even, "I don't think there's quite enough violence. We're not getting through to the kids."

I play all of them against each other, depending on what I think will work. Child's play.

I don't even have to be consistent in what I say; I only have to prey on each one's misgivings. Suggest here and there that I would be a more effective leader than he is.

I leave those suggestions out of my reports, though. The group's selecting me to replace Jones has to look natural to the team. It would never do for me to let The Company know my goal is to surpass my father's influence as a Project Paperclip asset. For my influence through Chrysalis to carry even more weight than his did—now *that* would be an accomplishment of which I could be proud.

They thought *he* was an asset! Well, they just hadn't yet met *me*.

❖❖ 10.2 BALTIMORE, 1968 ❖❖

THE CONTROL

I can't tell you how much I dread reporting the recent developments to Fleischer and The Company. While overall, the results are promising—kids do seem to be responding to the trauma protocol, with one boy in Maryland already deeply disturbed, and both the girls in Colorado exhibiting possible multiplicity—there is still nothing to report on any of the subjects in Bumblebee, and instead of splitting, each time I see Probity, she only seems more withdrawn.

On top of that, the whole Tennessee project seems to be imploding around Jones. He is out of control, completely depraved. I think he may be going mad. The protocol there has been thrown to the wind. Armleuchter is becoming progressively more violent. I'm afraid that if something isn't done soon, we may lose more than one subject at his hands.

He is clearly trying to orchestrate a *coup d'état*, when the only thing he was *supposed* to be doing was observing and reporting to Teufel's team what Jones was up to.

The whole thing is no more sturdy than a house of cards. A strong wind—hell, at this point even a gentle breeze—and it will all come falling down.

❖❖ 10.3 WASHINGTON, 1968 ❖❖

THE BUREAUCRAT

My head's on the chopping block if I have to take this to The Old Man.

My concerns have been increasing for a considerable time regarding the viability of the Tennessee project. The Colorado project is, at this point, our most successful. It looks as though our efforts with two of the kids there are working. One boy in Maryland is showing promise.

But Bumblebee. Oh, I had such great hopes for Bumblebee. It had everything going for it—location, leader, composition of the group. We thought we had a great setup there.

And now. Because of one damn child.

I cannot fathom what would have led Jones to kill one of our subjects. Up until recently, everything he has done has been calculated, cold. With the exception of choosing his own sacrifices, he has followed his directions meticulously.

But this! There is no explanation that makes sense other than he has simply lost control of himself and of the group. It is likely we are going to need to make some management changes there if anything is to be salvaged from Bumblebee at all. And damage control! Those parents are so distraught that at this point I'm not sure even blackmail will be enough to keep them quiet.

Perhaps the pilot projects have run their course. While they've been running, we've had time to search out new possibilities and we have a new crop of potential subjects large enough to support at least one test site in every state—actually, even more than that in most. We've gotten enough data back to finesse the protocol. We're about ready to begin the next round. When I talk to The Old Man I'll present it that way— that it is clearly time to put the next wave of projects into play.

❖❖ 10.4 BUMBLEBEE, 1968 ❖❖

GENT

Armleuchter's getting more dangerous. His behavior is more bizarre each time I see him, and his violence is escalating. His wife died this week in a fall. Even though it looks like an accident, I'm thinking it might have been suicide. Maybe even murder. If he didn't do it, I think he might have driven her to it. From the description of the scene, it could have gone either way.

Her wake and funeral services are set to take place in her hometown of Charlotte, North Carolina, this week. The wake is the night of Thursday, the 31st of October. The funeral's the next morning. That's the night of and the morning following our next meeting.

That should mean he'll be out of town with no practical way to get here and back in time. I can't see him flying here between services. That means he'll be gone Halloween. Perfect. Seeing as that's the biggest celebration of the year, instead of rescheduling it, I told him I couldn't miss it to attend the service. I simply told Meg we weren't going to go.

He's been stirring up discontent in the group for long enough. I know he is the one who is doing it. I listen. Nothing gets by me.

He thinks he could take it over, just pick up where I'd leave off. He has no idea what or who he's messing with. He has no idea at all.

As a result of the fortuitous connection between our families, I've been able to study him more closely than any other member of the group. I don't understand why they chose him to participate at all, given that he started out being in it just for the fun and the sex.

Every month, he has demonstrated an increasing obsession with violence. Not even the sex seems to provide him with the pleasure that blatant cruelty does.

He may be in it only for the fun, but I'll tell you what would be fun. What would be fun would be if the next sacrifice I had to offer for the cause was Armleuchter himself.

10.5 DETROIT, 1968

THE CONTROL

The Tennessee project is festering, like a giant boil coming to a head. I don't like it.

I've talked to Fleischer, but we can't figure out how to stop its downward spiral or get it back on track. On top of that, now Meg has called and says she wants to talk to me.

She says she wants to talk about something, work something out, but won't tell me what or why.

I'm in a precarious position there. Being around her clouds my thinking. I've wanted her since the first time I saw her—the first time she opened her mouth and began to sing.

But Fleischer has told me she's strictly off limits. Any inappropriate action on my part could jeopardize the project. There's too much at stake.

I've been able to keep my professional distance so far, as long as every interaction has been chaperoned by Jones. But she insists she has to meet me this time without him.

I suggested we meet at Union Station in Nashville. There's a restaurant there where we could get lost in the crowd. As long as we stay out in public, I think I'll be able to keep things under control.

10.6 WASHINGTON, 1968

THE RECRUITER

Martin, Fleischer, Teufel, and Jäger are supposed to meet next week to brainstorm about the crisis in Bumblebee. As a leader, Jones has turned out to be a miserable failure. He has murdered two locals that I'm sure of, and now possibly a third. He has killed one of our subjects. He can't keep members of his group under control. Fleischer is concerned that Armleuchter may need to be eliminated from the equation in order for equilibrium to be restored. I'm seriously considering the possibility that the one who needs to be neutralized may be Jones.

I am terribly disappointed. I am usually a much better judge of character than this. My mistake may have put the entire project in jeopardy.

If it has, the fate of my career may hang in the balance—more, the disposition of the entire project and even worse—the future of the country. They may all be at risk as a result of one lapse in judgment. Mine.

If I can figure out a way to do it, I need to take care of this problem myself. And before next week's meeting, if possible.

❖❖   10.7 BUMBLEBEE, 1968 ❖❖

MAMA

It happens every month on the full moon. I see that
now. I've gone back over schedules and calendars for
the past two years to put it all together, and every single
month without fail, Gent has made sure we're in
Bumblebee on the Saturday night closest to the full
moon. Halloween nights, too. Maybe other days, too; I
haven't figured it all out yet.

I know what will happen tonight because last
month on the Saturday closest to the full moon, I did
not drink the drink he handed me. I said I was tired and
went straight to bed. And when he sneaked out, I
followed him, taking the keys to his sleeping daddy's
Cadillac from the bowl by the front door.

When he got close to the place, I realized where he
must have been headed. I knew that clearing by the old,
abandoned church; he had taken me there to see the
place years ago, when we were not long married. I let
them get far enough ahead that they wouldn't be able to
hear me, parked alongside the road, and crept on alone
through the dark to the churchyard. All the leaves were
off the trees, so the light from their fire was more than
enough for me to be sure I was going in the right
direction.

From the shadows at the edge of the clearing, I
could see Gent hoisting Probity up in the air. He was
pulling a rope that went from one of her feet over the
branches of a large tree. Suddenly, I couldn't breathe. I

was gasping for air so desperately I was sure they would hear me.

I never realized till that moment how small that twelve-year-old child was, how frail. She was covered with bruises I had never seen because they had always been covered by clothes. I wanted to run to her, untie her, clutch her to me, get her out of there to safety, take her home. But I could do nothing. *Nothing.* I couldn't intervene because they would surely have killed us both. It was unbearable to watch, but I watched for long enough to be sure I had to wait, to figure out a plan.

Long enough to watch Gent torture and kill his best friend from childhood, as Billy sobbed and screamed for him to stop, begging Gent to tell him why. I could hear his answer, cold as ice, "You know what you did."

"I don't. I don't know why. What did I ever do to you?" Billy cried.

Gent leaned over and spoke directly into his ear, barely loud enough for me to make out over the echoes of the bees the town was named for, their resonance amplified by the hollow trees in which the bees lived, not far behind the church that hid me. From where I crouched, I heard his answer: "You made me want you, Billy; and then when I did, you didn't want me."

The month since then has been the longest month I've ever lived, knowing now what's been happening in my own house, under my own roof, being powerless to change it, living with a man I now know to be a murderer and a raper of children, pretending all was well.

It is not just that I am afraid of Gent, though I unquestionably am that, too. I am afraid of what he'd do if he thought I knew. I'm still an alien here, a citizen of France. My green card depends on my being married to a citizen; and if anything happened to me, *mon Dieu*, my children! What would happen to them if I was forced to leave the country, to leave them here with him?

So, I've waited throughout this terrible month. And I've plotted. And I've planned.

The hoods on their robes had hidden most of their faces, but in the firelight I was able to recognize one of them. His name is Leo; we've known him for years and have run into him many times when Gent and I have performed in Michigan, and a few other times in other places, too. He's always seemed so cultured and refined. What was *he* doing there, in the churchyard, from three states away? From how far did those people come? And how did they end up in *Bumblebee?*

At first glance, Gent appeared to be in charge, but the group didn't do anything without looking to Leo before they moved on. You could tell from watching the dynamics that Leo held the real power, and was for some unknown reason letting Gent act as though he was the group's leader instead. Gent was so excited he didn't notice.

They even had *announcements,* for heaven's sake, as though it were a meeting of the church council or a group of scout leaders instead! Next month, Gent said, the sacrifice would be something special. The implication was that tonight's sacrifice would be a human child.

Horrified, I watched another man, this one in a mask, cut the throat of a lamb, then pour its blood over the naked woman on the altar.

When the orgy started, unable to bear any more, I crept away and slunk home, like a kicked and beaten cur.

It took enormous courage, courage I never knew I possessed, to call Leo, to go to talk to him and tell him that I knew, that it had to stop. But I'd have risked anything to protect my daughter. In fact, I *did* risk everything to do what I thought I had to do to make it stop.

Crée en moi un cœur pur, ô mon Dieu! Please give me a pure heart—and the strength to do whatever it is I must.

❖❖ 10.8 BUMBLEBEE, 1968 ❖❖

GENT

How I ended up in this position, I'm not quite sure; no one has bothered to share that information with me. But clearly someone in this group sold me out for their own thirty pieces of silver, whatever that reward might be for them, and I'm not in a position now to find out why.

It's not as though I don't know what I've done to deserve this. Nothing I could say or do now would make any difference in what's going to happen to me, or when. Knowing who did it and why wouldn't really change a thing.

At this moment, it's hard to tell exactly what is going on, which character is playing what role in this drama. They took my glasses when they stripped me, so I can't see very far. Everything beyond a few feet is a blur of color and motion. I'd never thought before now about how not having her glasses would make everything look to Probity. I don't know why it didn't occur to me until just this moment that perhaps this is why we could never get her to break. Maybe all this time we've been putting on our show for someone who never got the full benefit from it simply because she couldn't see it at all.

Still, I can follow the majority of the ritual easily enough by heart. By heart, that's a joke. Soon, I'll be the one losing mine. But until then, the process is fascinating to follow. There is a heightened sense of excitement among the group tonight. Or perhaps, then again, maybe it's just my own.

If Armleuchter pulled this off, I'd have thought he'd have made a point of scheduling his wife's memorial service so he could be here instead of out of town, so I don't think he was the one. Then again, maybe the fact that everyone thinks he's there is the perfect alibi and he flew here after all.

At any rate, at least one of the group must have been complicit in Probity's absence from the circle at the moment I was surrounded, because I haven't been able to identify her presence since. I'm not sure what that means. I can't begin to discern if her being here would have made any difference at all. Would they not have taken me in front of her? Would she have joined in, or fought against them? Would her being here have changed anything at all? Does the observer change, simply by existing and observing, the action being observed?

Philosophical questions, all of them, the answers to which don't mean a thing.

If they really understood how much is at stake, they *would* have her here, have *her* hold the knife. Perhaps that is their intention. I wonder if they will. Maybe then, this will be the night I've waited for all along. Maybe my death will be the catalyst it would take for her to shatter into the separate pieces we've worked for all these years. Maybe then I really would be a sacrifice for a cause greater than myself. I'd be a hero after all.

At any rate, tonight it is clearly my turn to die. I am the one who lies here, trussed up like next month's

Thanksgiving turkey awaiting the carving knife: bound, gagged, and naked on this rock we've used all this time as an altar, but which I can see from where I am now is nothing more than a rough chunk of stone. The rock is surprisingly cold against my back. Body heat isn't enough to warm it, even the part that directly touches skin. I never noticed that before. It won't be much longer now.

It is curious, though, what they say about your whole life flashing before your eyes when you're about to die. That isn't what I am experiencing at all. All I can see is that hallway and Deed and Si and myself as boys. And I know that shortly, *I'll* be the one who gets pushed out a window while I'm still looking out at an unfinished life. Not as innocent as Deed was then, but still. Soon I'll look up and see the eyes of tonight's knife wielder coming towards me, and it will be me hitting the sidewalk down below instead of Deed; it will be my own life, by my own doing if not by my own hand, that will be undone.

Here comes the robe toward me. The horned mask approaches; the knife.

Oh, my. Now that's a surprise. I know those eyes. Tonight isn't about what I thought it was after all.

Death comes for me now, and with it comes unlimited power in the knowledge that my light is about to be extinguished.

At this moment, as I die, for the first time in my entire life, I feel completely alive.

CHAPTER ELEVEN

11.1 BUMBLEBEE, 1968

MAMA

We never speak of that night, Probity and I. It's almost as though it never happened, except it must have—because at some point, Leo delivered her to me, and Gent is dead and gone. I'm not even sure she was aware I was there by the time she got home. She was in some sort of trance and didn't speak at first, but I guided her to her room where she collapsed onto her bed. Immediately, it seemed, she fell asleep. He must have done that with her before. If I could've picked her up and carried her to her bed I would have. Maybe he did that, too.

I'm not sure, but I don't think she remembers anything. The next morning I let the children sleep in, and when they awoke I told them Gent had died the night before. I said that after they went to bed, he ran out to the store to get something for breakfast, crashed his car into a pole, and died. That's all they ever need to know.

Leenie has come down from New York to be with us. The past few days have been the first time I can ever remember her telling me how proud she is of me. She said she's amazed at how I'm picking up the pieces and soldiering on. I even heard her say to someone at the funeral, "I don't know how that sister of mine does it! It must be those Stellaire genes we inherited from our parents. We should all have such spine!" Our whole lives, it seems, she's been bossing me around and treating me like the little sister, and now, of all times, she's proud of me. After all the years of Gent telling me I was doing everything wrong, it means the world to me that she now thinks I'm doing well. I can't tell you how much it helps.

The only thing to do now is put it behind us, pick up our lives, and carry on. In order to assure our survival, I must never speak of any of these things again, not even in confession. I do not dare.

11.2 BUMBLEBEE, 1969

PROBITY, AGE THIRTEEN

I sure do miss my Granddaddy, but I've never yet been able to work myself up to feeling too bad about Papa. Granddaddy died just a few days after Papa did. Grandmomma said he died of a broken heart. They said Papa probably had a heart attack while driving, ran into a telephone pole, and the car caught on fire. Nothing but a few bones left to bury. Nothing, really, to even say goodbye to.

They had a big service and all for each of them. Papa's was on the day before Granddaddy died. Not so many people came to Granddaddy's funeral, but I liked his better. At least on the day of his, it wasn't raining like it was for Papa's. Granddaddy was always kind to me, and I don't remember Papa ever being kind to me if somebody wasn't looking, not once. I never even really thought about him being kind at all.

It wasn't 'til today that I heard the story about Papa and the dead bird.

After school started this year, I was able to get a work permit for the drive-in, as long as I work a short schedule 'cause I am so young. So today, I was working as the soda jerk when one of the local police officers came up to the window and ordered a large grape slush. While I was making it for him, he started telling me about something that had happened years ago, when he was just a boy.

Turns out they were all just sitting there, a bunch of boys of different ages with their daddies, waiting on a Saturday morning to get their hair cut at the only barber shop in town, when they saw Papa out the big plate-glass window, walking down the other side of the street. The officer said there was a dead bird lying in the gutter, hit by a car or something. And Papa, he said, stopped and bent down and stroked that bird like he felt sorry for it, or like it was hurt or something and he was just petting it to try to make it feel better, and then he stood back up and kept on walking.

The officer was telling me about it like it was a good memory that ought to make me feel better about my daddy being dead and all, and how kind he had been to even little dead creatures. But instead, all I thought on the inside was, *I sure wish he'd been that nice to me.*

❖❖ 11.3 ATLANTA, 1969 ❖❖

THE MOLE

I wasn't there the night Gent Jones died, and I am furious Teufel didn't tell me what was going to happen. The least he could have done was let me know there was a change in the plan. Even if they didn't mean for me to be the one who got to kill him, if I had known what was in the works, I'd have figured out a way to change their minds.

It must have been glorious! I'd have given anything for the chance to see my greatest rival dead and cold and bloody on the slab. To have held the knife in my hands would have been perfect. Surely then the leadership of the group would have automatically fallen to me.

Instead, for the time being, Leo Niadh has that honor. But I know how I can get my revenge. He has wanted Meg for years, so I'm going after her. He'll be sorry he ever crossed me. She'll be mine alone.

Both our spouses are newly in the grave, but I've already started courting her. Calling to "make sure she's okay," and to "see if she and the children need anything." If I can't have the group, I'll take what he wants most. Everyone is bound to think, *oh, isn't that nice,* a grieving widow, a grieving widower… and within a few months, if I work it right, she'll be mine.

❖❖   11.4 Bumblebee, 1969 ❖❖

Probity, Age Thirteen

"It feels like my heart is plum breakin'." My granddaddy used to say that sometimes, and I didn't know then what he meant, but I do now. Now I know *exactly* what he meant.

Mama has decided to marry Armleuchter. And he's a bad man, a very bad man, the worst. The problem is, he makes her happy. To hear her describe him, he's smart, and well educated, and cultured, and rich, and he's Catholic on top of all, and that's important to her, too. She doesn't know him like I do.

Even though everyone else always calls him by his last name, she's always called him by his first name, Luke. But lately, she doesn't even call him that anymore; she's nicknamed him Lucky. But he'll never be lucky for me. He has the right name for what I think of him already—in German, his name is slang for asshole. And he's not just an *armleuchter*; he's a *kronleuchter!* A giant asshole!

Papa and Granddaddy haven't even been dead a year and Ernie's hardly ever home from college, and Grandmomma has decided that if Armleuchter is moving in, she's moving out. I'm losing everybody, all of them at once. My heart is just breaking. I can't bear it. And there's no way I can tell Mama.

I tried once. I told her I didn't want Armleuchter to live here with us. It was breakfast time and we were sitting at the kitchen table and I told her I hated being around him, 'cause when I am, I feel like a slut. She asked me if I knew what that meant, but when I said yes she didn't even ask me why I felt that way. She just went right on eating her breakfast.

Even I can see she's been sad for too long, and now she's happy. Love has blinded her. I can't tell her now.

Soon Mama has to go out and finish this year's concert season all alone, without Papa to accompany her. She has to. The concerts were already booked. She found a new accompanist and they've been practicing, so she'll be gone soon. And Ernie and Grandmomma will be gone, too, and while Mama's on the road that *kronleuchter* will be staying here with Equity and me. I know what he wants. And I know no matter what you do, he will hurt you to get it.

Whatever it takes, I have to protect Equity. There's no one else here to do it, so that's my job now. The monsters never come to get her in the night, so she hasn't ever been hurt yet, and I don't want her to ever have to feel like I do inside. Whatever he wants me to do, I'll do it, if he'll just leave her alone.

11.5 Bumblebee, 1969

Mama

Within the first nine months after Gent's death, Probity and Equity and I lived through enough chaos and pain and wonder for a lifetime.

It seemed only days after Gent's and his daddy's funerals that Luke Armleuchter started calling. He lived in Atlanta, just a few hours away, and he and his wife and Gent and I had been friends for years. They had moved to the States at the same time as Luke's father, a German scientist, after the war. Luke was, I guess, Gent's best friend. That should have been the first warning sign I heeded.

But I didn't. He was European, aristocratic, educated, cultured. He loved music and art and literature, and he was lonely, as I was, too. He said all the right things at all the right times. And with Gent and his daddy and Earnest all gone, Probity and Equity needed a man in their lives. After all the years of Gent's abuse, I stretched towards Luke like a plant hidden too long from the sun. In no time at all I fell for him, hook, line, and sinker.

We were married just a few months after Gent's death, on May Day. Luke insisted on it, saying the day held special significance for him, though he never did tell me what it was. By that time, though, there was no mistaking my pregnancy for anything other than what it was. I must have conceived on the very day of Gent's death, and though I kept thinking I was a little old for that, there we were, newlyweds, all excited, with a new baby coming. Luke had never had children of his own, and welcomed the baby as though it was his first. It seemed too good to be true.

And it was.

Within days after the wedding, it was Gent all over again. Luke started yelling at me. He hit me one time, then many, always saying it was my fault, and eventually I realized that perhaps his first wife hadn't been as clumsy as he'd led everyone to believe. I began to wonder if her death was not accidental, but murder. Still, I was sure he wouldn't hurt the children. It was me he was angry with, not them.

But then little things started falling together quickly, like dominoes. I came back home from the road to discover that Probity had started wearing makeup. I realized within days it was to hide bruises. He said things that sounded suspiciously familiar, like phrases I'd heard the night I followed Gent to the woods. At first I thought maybe he had heard them from Gent. But even though I didn't think I had seen him there the same night I followed Gent, I realized that at some point he must have been there, too, perhaps behind the mask.

In the end, I realized I had done it again. I had married a second husband who was just like the first. Maybe worse.

My learning curve was much steeper the second time around. I realized that I didn't—that abused women don't—notice the abuse as quickly as their friends and family members because they are in the middle of it. If you met a man who walked up to you on the street and struck you, you'd likely call the police—and I would, too. But if the man is more subtle, if he takes his time, if he starts out saying sweet nothings, gradually slides into saying things that hurt your feelings, but then apologizes and promises he won't do it again, you think it was an accident, so you give him another chance. If he says something cruel, but then buys you roses and apologizes and says he didn't mean to hurt you and won't do it again, you believe that, too, and you give him another chance.

If he behaves in a threatening manner but then tells you *I'm sorry I scared you, baby,* and says he won't do it again, you give him another chance. Maybe by then you're feeling physically afraid of him and are wishing you could get out, but you've been pretending that everything is okay for so long you're sure everyone else believes the illusion of your happy relationship; and he's made you doubt yourself for so long you believe him that it's all your fault, so when he hits you the first time you are too ashamed to tell anyone the truth; and when he says he didn't *want* to hit you but it's your fault because *you just made him so mad,* you believe that, too, so you give him another chance.

When you tell him your concerns about the state of your relationship, he belittles and blames you until you think you're making a big thing out of nothing, so you give him another chance. When he drives all your friends away, controls the family's finances and all of their movements and decisions, you don't think you're worth rescuing anymore, so you give him another chance.

When he bullies you into doing whatever he says by threatening your children and you're afraid he will hurt them, and sometimes he does, you give him another chance.

And then, when your friends and family members tell you they are concerned about you, and that they can see what is happening whether you deny it or you do not, he tells you *they* are the ones trying to control you; and by that time you are too afraid to leave even if they come bringing suitcases to help you pack your bags and take you somewhere safe, because you are already so damaged you believe it when he tells you no one else will ever love you like he does, and that he will hunt you down and hurt you, no matter where you go, so you give him another chance. And eventually, you give him one last chance, and he takes the life you've placed over and over again in his hands.

Wherever you are in that cycle, I learned, it is *always* the right time to stop giving him another chance.

When I realized I'd fallen for a man like that again, I decided I'd been able to get out once and I was never going to be in that position again. Luke had hurt us for the last time. He had used up his last chance.

I told Probity that if he ever hit anyone again, she was to call the police. And the next time he started hitting me, she did.

They arrested Luke and took him to jail, but when he started telling stories of devils and orgies and sacrifices, then, as all things eventually do, the situation revealed its funny side. Instead of believing him, they transferred him over to Central State Hospital for the Insane, just east of Nashville.

Once there, he not only repeated everything he had told the police, but also added that he was descended from royalty, an aristocrat. That made them up his diagnosis from "paranoid schizophrenic with psychotic episodes" to "paranoid schizophrenic with psychotic episodes and delusions of grandeur" as well. Far be it from me to be the one to tell them that everything he'd said to them was true.

The poetically-just result was that because of his violence to me, the investigation into his first wife's death was reopened. I was told that he confessed during his interrogation, screaming that she had deserved it. He only wished, he said, that he'd been able to offer her as a sacrifice. Through some finagling, his attorneys were able to negotiate his incarceration for life, not in prison, where he belonged, but at a Georgia institution for the criminally insane, since it was closer to his home. They thought he'd get more visitors that way.

I don't know if he ever had a single one before he died. If he did, it wasn't I.

If I had told them the truth, they'd have believed I was crazy. Since he did, they locked him away.

Luke's defilement of our home seemed to drag out forever, but it was actually within three months of the wedding that Probity called the police. With his incarceration, the girls and I were finally free. As quickly as I could make it happen, the three of us moved from the farmhouse into something smaller, a move that was completed only days before Asset's birth. And with that new beginning, Probity, Equity, Asset, and I all started our lives anew.

11.6 DETROIT, 1970

THE CONTROL

What a mess. I've been working with the state legislature down there in Tennessee, trying to get our bill passed, while at the same time trying to clean up all the chaos Jones left behind. Covering all of our asses, and dispersing the Bumblebee group members to other sites. It's reminded me of President Roosevelt's great words about his daughter, Alice: "I can be President of the United States, or I can control Alice. I cannot possibly do both."

The drive down there and back is killing me. If it weren't for the opportunity to see Meg occasionally, I'd ask them to get someone local to take care of it. But even the rare glance over a cup of coffee makes it worthwhile.

I don't think I'll ever get over the powerful longing I have for her. The rest of it was just the job. Didn't much care for a lot of it, but it was the job. But Meg was different. That was for me. And then, too, there was arranging for The Company to facilitate Armleuchter's life sentence in the loony bin. That one was for Probity alone.

The Company says to cut our losses, let it go. If they transfer my assignment to another project, I'll have to take it. And if that happens, I won't be able to sneak back to see Meg. They would know. They always know. There is always one more person than you think watching your back. And then there's someone else, watching his.

11.7 BUMBLEBEE, 1971

PROBITY, AGE FIFTEEN

When I was really small and Grandmomma had her first stroke, it left her with only one side of her face working and she was a little scary looking. After that, she would take her false teeth out and shake her head till her cheeks wiggled like Richard Nixon's and laugh like the Wicked Witch of the West so we would laugh, too, and wouldn't be afraid of her. She taught me to sew and liked to do jigsaw puzzles with me, and I never doubted she loved me, not even once; and she used to make me laugh even more than the Wicked Witch when everybody in our family would get in those big arguments about being Republicans and Democrats and politics and such, and whenever anyone would ask her how *she* voted she'd wink at me and say, "One of my favorite things about living in the United States, Little Bit, is that we have a secret ballot, and no one person has to *ever* tell any other person how they voted." I always believed that meant she was a Democrat and wasn't going to ever tell Granddaddy. I still do.

My favorite thing she ever said to me was, "Things are not beautiful in and of themselves. They are merely keys which unlock the beauty hiding inside *you*."

Isn't that an amazing thing to say? Golly, she was wonderful to me. I miss her something awful.

Grandmomma died last week while I was out on a date with boy I really like. There was the most magnificent lightning storm I ever saw, and the boy and

I sat out in his car in a cornfield and necked while it was going on.

Then, when I got back home, I found out Grandmomma had died while I was gone. I'm so sorry I didn't go to the hospital that night to be with her instead. Maybe she came by to say goodbye to me in the lightning.

I loved Grandmomma. And I love Mama, and I love Aunt Leenie, too. Aunt Leenie's tough, like me, but Mama's not. I know it's my responsibility to take care of Mama now. It was my grandparents who always made me feel like they were there to take care of me.

I know I don't need to worry as much about taking care of everybody else now that Gent is dead and Armleuchter is locked up. They're saying he'll never get out, and that makes me feel a little better. But the truth is, I don't even like him being alive. Just his being *alive* at the same time I am makes the world feel too small. There's one part of it I really do like, though. Being 'round him made me feel crazy. And now he's the one locked up 'cause they think he really is. I guess that's the best I can hope for.

But if I have to take care of Mama and Equity and Brother, and Grandmomma and Granddaddy and Ernie are all gone, who's left to take care of me?

11.8 WASHINGTON, 2014

THE BUREAUCRAT

Just as Operation Paperclip—which began in 1945—led to Projects Chatter (1947), Bluebird (1951-53), and Artichoke (1951-53), all of those preceded MKNaomi (1953-70) and MKUltra—which officially ran from 1953 to 1963. Some say MKUltra spawned Monarch, which metamorphosed into Chrysalis. The Company publicly denies this claim. It is our official position that the last two never happened. We are confident that no one will ever be able to prove otherwise.

By 1963, the name of the program had been changed to Project Search, which ran until 1973. After Search ended, Project Stargate ran until 1984, at which time it became the current operation, the name of which remains classified. If the new program doesn't work, we'll shut that down, too, cover it up, start something new, and try again.

The most frustrating aspect of the entire operation is that it appears there are others who have already developed a protocol which is working for them, and they are using it against us. In December of 2014, something we've been trying to hide for years finally hit the news: *The Torture Report* revealed that not one of the torture techniques we've been using all this time under the provisions of the Homeland Security Act has provided us with the kinds of intelligence information we've been hoping for. No matter how violent, how humiliating, how traumatic, how degrading our forms of torture are, we have been unable to break many of our detainees, and when we have broken them, the information we have gained has not proven to be reliable. Whether our efforts at producing the same results in our own spies have been as successful—an issue on which I am not willing to comment—it is clear that others have already achieved the result we have been working towards—officially, at least—since 1947. Since we have been training insurgents in a number of foreign countries for decades, our frustration now may be of our own doing.

Off the record, we've been quietly working at cleaning up the mess Chrysalis left for quite some time, primarily discrediting the surviving subjects and the doctors who treat them. Some say we're behind the False Memory Syndrome Foundation, but whether we are or are not, I'll never tell. The group does good work, though, planting seeds of doubt wherever and whenever someone claims to remember something which might paint us in a bad light. I am confident they'll never be able to prove we're connected with the FMSF movement, either.

I've even heard some folks say that it is *we* who should be diagnosed with something they're calling the False *Innocence* Belief Syndrome (FIBS), but other than its being a catchy acronym, it is fortunately an idea that has never caught on. I don't anticipate ever seeing it being added to the Diagnostic and Statistical Manual of Mental Disorders (the DSM) in any upcoming version.

The bottom line is that we really expected we'd be in the clear by now. We believed all the records had been destroyed, but then after time passed and files of that age were declassified, some were discovered to have accidentally escaped The Old Man's directive. We thought all the subjects had been successfully programmed to self-destruct before they would reveal anything that happened, but far too many have now overcome their programming to reveal what was meant to be kept silent. We should have been protected by laws that would have prohibited the arrest and prosecution of child abuse perpetrators after the child turned nineteen, but some states have since revoked or amended those laws.

We thought we had eliminated all the evidence, terrified the children into silence, smothered their memories, and covered all the bases on the long shot that we were ever found out. But in spite of our best efforts, the older the subjects have become, the more they have ended up in doctors' and therapists' offices all across the country, telling stories that sound suspiciously alike.

We remain confident, however, that no one—*no one*—will ever be able to prove any of it.

11.9 BUMBLEBEE, 1971

EQUITY

I'm disappointed that Probity is always so angry with our father. It doesn't make any sense to me. She's always saying bad things about Papa, but he wasn't a bad man at all. I wish she wouldn't put me in the middle, feeling like I have to defend his memory. She doesn't realize that when she says bad things about him, that if I am half him and half Mama, she's saying bad things about me, too.

I miss him every day. Probity spent more time with Grandmomma and Granddaddy than I ever did, so she misses them more, but I was always Daddy's Little Girl. He was funny and kind to me, and he was handsome, too. He was smart and charming and whenever he'd pick me up or put his arms around me, I just knew that everything was going to be okay. I loved playing duets on the piano with him, even though she didn't. He and I had a lot in common.

Ernie is right. Probity always makes a big deal out of everything. She's always been so serious. Always acting like *she* was the mama. She acts like she carries the burdens of the world. She should lighten up. We're still just kids! She *is* making a big deal out of everything! Feeling bad doesn't change anything at all. She's always so unhappy she makes everyone around her unhappy, too. I refuse to be. I choose to be happy. I just want her to be able to be happy, too.

❖❖ 11.10 BUMBLEBEE, 1971 ❖❖

Mama

Everybody tells me Asset looks just like me. I don't know about that, but he sure doesn't look like anybody else in the family *except* for me. He has always been mine. Just mine.

I know you're not supposed to have favorites, but I love that little boy more than I ever thought possible. I just can't help myself.

It's been almost two years now since Asset was born. He's as old now as Deed was when he died. Born too soon after Armleuchter and I married for him to be the product of my second marriage, everyone just assumed he was Gent's. It had, after all, been exactly the right amount of time since Gent died. He could have been Asset's father. And by the time I knew I was pregnant, Gent was already dead and wasn't around to tell anyone he hadn't touched me that way in years.

My Asset. Everyone thought I named him out of respect for Gent's daddy, just carrying on the tradition of real estate names. But that wasn't it, you know. No one has ever known—no one *must* ever know—that wasn't the type of asset for which I named him.

I named him for the only asset I had that Leo would trade for, in exchange for the chance to wear a robe and a mask one night only, and the right to wield the knife.

CHAPTER TWELVE

12.1 Nashville, 2015

Probity

After Gent died and Armleuchter was locked up, we moved out of the farmhouse I grew up in. For a long time after that, I couldn't remember a thing that happened before the move. It was as though when the front door swung shut on our old house, another door had swung shut in my mind, so silent there wasn't a clang or a bang or even a creak to bring your attention to the fact that something had just happened. It just quietly closed all my past away. When I'd look back, nothing.

I knew enough stories to get by. Anytime anyone asked about my childhood, I'd trot out one of those stories about the time we were this place or that, about some bit of family history I'd memorized, or stories, mostly, that I'd heard others tell about me. But I couldn't see them, hear them, taste them. No actual memory at all.

Every once in a while I'd listen to someone else tell something that had happened to them when they were small, and it would always take me by surprise. It was only at those times that I ever even *thought* about the fact that other people seemed to be able to remember things that had happened to them, and I, I alone, could not.

It wasn't until after my own son, L.B., was born that I started thinking I was going crazy. His daddy and I had gotten married right out of high school and were already separated by the time he was born, four years later. I was still doing fine as a single mother right up until L.B.'s first Halloween, when he was just a few months old. When the night finally came, instead of opening the door for the neighborhood kids, I locked the two of us in the apartment, turned out all of the lights, and hid with him in my room. All night long I was terrified he would make a sound, that someone would hear him and know we were in there and find us. I honestly don't know what I'd have done if someone had.

In my mind, neither of us was safe, and I had no idea why. Then there was nothing, a blank again, for the next several years.

When L.B. got to be about the age that I was then, back when it all started, that's when the memories started breaking through. Flashbacks of the reality behind the nightmares, mostly, at first the ones I'd had all of my life. But when he was just a boy they started changing.

Up until then I'd had only two. Same two nightmares every night. Two o'clock in the morning, I'd wake up. Heart pounding, cold sweating, couldn't get away. *Got to get away.* Couldn't get away. Didn't dare go back to sleep because the bad guys might come and get me while I slept.

Only the two. The same two nightmares every single night for my whole life, up until L.B. was as old as I was then. That's when they started getting worse.

12.2 NASHVILLE, 1995

L.B.

It started when I was about five or six, I guess. I'd hear her sometimes, downstairs crying in the middle of the night. Sometimes before the sobbing started, from all the way upstairs I'd hear her crying out. *Please, don't. Please, stop. Please, hurry. I'll be good. I promise. This time, I'll be good.*

Then, after a while, it started sooner and sooner after I went to bed. Sometimes once it started, it would last until daylight.

Other times, I would see her crying in the car, silent tears running down her cheeks when she thought I wasn't looking. It seemed she was sad all the time.

Then one night, *I* was the one who woke up screaming. I still remember the dream. She was dead. I had to go live with some friends of ours, and leave my school and my friends, and she was dead. When I started screaming, she came into my room, picked me up and held me, rocking me in the rocking chair we hardly ever used anymore, until finally, I fell asleep again. The next morning was the first time she called Doc.

When I left for college, she told me she remembered that night, too. She'd been planning to kill herself, she said, in so much pain she'd forgotten about everyone else in the world, including me. She'd forgotten about everybody, except for them. "The bad guys," she called them, whoever they were. But when I woke up crying, she remembered me. She said I saved her life. And though she would never have asked for help for herself, the next morning she sought help because she wanted to live for me.

12.3 Nashville, 2015

Probity

Eventually, the nightmares broke into the daytimes, and I realized that I couldn't tell the good guys from the bad guys anymore. In my head it was all jumbled together and it felt like my entire self was being ripped apart, limb from limb, every time a new memory was trying to get out. First the nightmares would change. I'd have a new one, then that one would mutate, night after night, until finally it turned into flashbacks of a new memory that came even when I was awake. I can't tell you how much I hated them. The memories, I mean. I was too afraid of the bad guys to hate *them*. I hated myself instead.

It felt like my body was erupting, my skin splitting open, like the memories were being ripped out of me by force. And then they started coming closer and closer together until there wasn't even time to recover from one before the next one hit.

Somewhere in there's when I started going to see Doc. I called the first time when I realized the only place Gent and the rest of the bad guys were still alive was in my memory, and killing myself to get to them was seeming like a better and better idea all the time. By the time I got to Doc, I couldn't tell what was real from what was crazy, and I thought being crazy was a better option than believing what I feared *might* be real, really was.

For the next few years, it seemed like each and every memory was worse than the one before, but always, every time, there was an overwhelming sense of dread; it always felt like something else worse was still coming, and I didn't want to know what it was. And it kept up like that, getting worse and worse, until I finally got to the memory of the Halloween when I was seven. After that I'd still remember something new now and then, but it was never worse than that one. Only variations on a theme I'd heard before.

After a while, looking back was like someone took a big box of Polaroid snapshots and threw them all up in the air, where they got caught by the wind so when they finally landed on the ground some were face up, some were face down, and some were missing altogether. Once the horror of what was in the ones I could see started to abate, I started trying to put them all in order, and to figure out what was on the flipsides of the ones that didn't show. I asked Mama, who asked Ernie and Equity, if they looked back and saw the same things I did, too, but they said they didn't.

Trying to line those photos up was like connecting the dots in a coloring book and trying to guess what the picture of my life would've been, if only someone else hadn't come along and erased more than half the dots I needed before I even had a chance to begin.

12.4 NASHVILLE, 1989

MAMA

Probity is falling apart. I'm not sure exactly what is happening, but she is telling me—and she's telling other people—things that simply cannot be true. They must not be true. I won't let them.

Last week, with Probity's consent, I went to see her doctor. I admitted nothing. I couldn't risk it. I can't even risk admitting what happened to myself. Only Leo knows I was the one under the robe and mask after we traded places the night Gent died, and he would die a thousand deaths before he would betray me. To this day, I have never told another soul what happened that night, and I swear I never will.

So I admitted nothing to Probity's doctor—or to myself. All I could do was assure myself that she is in good hands. And I let him know it would take less time for him to treat her *as though* it had happened than it would to convince her it did not.

It was the best that I could do.

12.5 NASHVILLE, 2015

PROBITY

There's no point in telling you all the things I remembered before it was over. It'd probably only make me feel bad and you feel worse. And telling it wouldn't change anything anyway.

You sure don't need to know all the horrible ways they could kill, the ways they could torture and maim not just bodies, but our spirits, too. But it is important to me to tell you about those who died. To acknowledge their lives were lived and cut short. To say aloud that even the bad guys couldn't eradicate them completely from the face of the earth, because every time I think of them they are not forgotten. Their deaths will be remembered as long as I, and now you, breathe.

I suspect there were more I still don't remember; certainly there were others who died in places other than Bumblebee, people I never knew, who lived and whose lives were taken in places I've never been. But these are the ones whose memories I bear. When I go to my own grave, please remember them for me, and help keep them alive as they deserved to have been.

I truly don't wish to give you nightmares or pass my trauma on to you, so if you're easily haunted by painful images just skip the next page. Take my word for it. Don't even argue. Just shut your eyes, skip over the fine print, say a prayer for all the victims, and turn the page.

The images that haunt me are these:

❖ The dark old man with the salt'n'pepper hair, who was so afraid he kept falling down. Sometimes in my mind's eye he's sitting on the curb, while other times he's tied up to the trunk of a tree while his throat is being cut, making it gurgle like a bubbling hose.

❖ The unsuspecting group member who lost the bizarre take-off on duck-duck-goose, who was strangled with a piano wire someone had fastened onto sticks.

❖ The little boy in the yellow shirt and the green shorts, whose head was smashed into the big stone in the middle of the clearing for no other reason than because he was playing when we were supposed to be quiet.

❖ The bare man who was tied to the post, and whose skin was pulled off bit by bit with pliers until he finally screamed himself into silence.

❖ The hitchhiker they burned alive in the fire.

❖ The woman who was kind to me because I was scared, so they cut her up and put her in a big tub of water, where her hair floated in the blood and water, looking like spaghetti in sauce. And then they put me in there with her and held me under the water, too, to make sure I knew it could happen to me.

❖ The two not-yet-born babies who didn't survive.

❖ The one whose memory has been obscured in my mind by age, fear, and worry about all those who suffered at the hands of the bad guys, and who has come to represent to me all those whose names and circumstances I didn't ever know.

❖ And the infant who was stabbed in the heart.

I still don't know their names. But I remember them, each and every one. And though they may not have been killed for their political beliefs, it *was* because of international politics that they died.

So for each and every one of those who disappeared, I speak as they answer at the feast for the dead:

"*¡Presente!*" for them, and for me, and for you.

DEED

I only wanted
        to see my mother,
                but there were clouds,
                        and there were birds,
                                and there were trees.

                        As I fell
                from the window,
                there were voices.
                I heard them all
                as I spun
                in the breeze.

Si said: *Put him down!*
                Let him be!

        Gent said: *It's your fault!*
                You should've stopped me!

                Mother said: *Oh, my God!*
                        Somebody catch him!
                                Help him please!

12.7 NASHVILLE, 2015

PROBITY

After all the memories started taking over my head, I could hardly function for the longest time. It was all I could do to go to work and take care of L.B.

I'm not even sure how I survived those years, when I could barely get up out of bed in the morning, much less put one foot in front of the other or go to work or fix my only living child something to eat. But I did. And we survived.

I may have been dying on the inside, hoping every day somebody or something would kill me or that I was dying for real, but in all that time I never missed a day of work, and I always made sure L.B. was fed and made it to school and whatever other sports and activities he was scheduled to attend. Somehow, against all odds, day after day, we survived. To this day I don't know how.

I'm right sure I'd never have made it without Doc. Every time I thought I was drowning in memories and feelings and fear, like there was no lifeline I could grab hold of, so bad I couldn't breathe, he'd be there in my mind, or in his office, or on the other end of the phone, saying even if I felt like I was drowning, I was really still safe, because he said he knew how to swim. When I thought I'd never make it, he reminded me he'd accompanied other folks on that long and treacherous journey before.

To help pay for therapy, I applied for financial assistance from the Victims of Crime Act (VOCA), which provides funding for crime-related expenses through our state's Criminal Injury Compensation Fund.

The fear of filling out the forms was darn near paralyzing all by itself. Writing it all down meant I was saying I really believed all that stuff really happened. You had to swear to it when you signed your name. Oh, God help me. Maybe I wasn't crazy after all and all that stuff really did happen. Some days I still can't decide which option—real or crazy—would be worse.

So, I filled out all the forms and wrote down the least of everything I'd remembered up until then that would make my needing therapy make sense, and signed my name. Sent them all in with a letter from Doc explaining why it took me so long to apply, why it was over a dozen years past the deadline and I'd just then been able to bring myself to write it all down and send it in. See, for crimes that happen to a child, the deadline for applying is a year after the victim's eighteenth birthday, and by that time I was way past thirty.

That part made no sense to me at all. How can there be a deadline for telling someone what happened when you were a child, when sometimes you can't remember? You'd think that instead of setting deadlines we couldn't meet, they'd be gratefully paying us retroactive combat pay plus interest, instead, for all the years our lives were lived in battle zones of their making. And for those of us walking wounded who *survived* the trauma they inflicted, they ought to pay us disability, too, for all the damage that was done to us, instead of just pretending we don't exist at all. Even the

church has to pay for abuse perpetrated by its priests.
Sure seems to me the USA ought to have to do the
same, for actions taken by its CIA.

Anyway, the criteria for Criminal Injury Compensation was this: You had to have suffered personal
injury from a violent crime, and you couldn't have
contributed to the crime in any way. You had to have a
good reason if you hadn't reported the crime within
forty-eight hours. For me, that was because I was just a
kid. You had to have cooperated with law enforcement
so they could investigate and prosecute the bad guys.
You had to have filed your claim within a year of the
crime or the time you stopped being a minor. That I
hadn't was what that letter from Doc was for.

I eventually got a letter back in the mail that said
the District Attorney's office had investigated, and had
determined that the crimes really had occurred and that
I met all the requirements, but that they didn't have to
pay for any crime that happened before the Act was
voted into existence and signed off on by Reagan in
1984. By the time I got to that part, my eyes had
already gone on to read the next line, but my brain was
still stuck on re-reading the line before.

They said it really happened.

12.8 Savannah, 2015

Asset

Probity seems to think I don't know that something bad happened to her before I was born, but I'm not stupid. I know she still sees me as her baby brother, but I'm not a child any more.

I'm a grown man, almost forty-five years old now, for Pete's sake. I've got kids older than she must have been then, one grandkid who must be close, and I'm big enough now to protect them if they need it. I read the papers, watch the news. I know some people do horrible things to children. I've read those descriptions the schools send home about how to tell if your child is using drugs, or has a learning disorder, or has been abused. In Probity's case I may not know exactly what happened, but I know enough to know something did, and to know that it was bad. I know she was hurt. I know she still carries her burden alone.

I wish she wouldn't. I hope that someday soon, she'll trust me with it. Whenever she does, I'm ready.

When the time comes, I'm going to tell her I believe her. Even more than that, I believe *in* her. Maybe she's not ready to trust me with it just yet, or maybe she doesn't want to. Maybe she just can't. It really doesn't matter. I'm a patient man.

You know, she may be my big sister, but there's a part of Probity that is still like my daughters, just like a little girl inside. I know how I'd feel if someone hurt my girls. I feel that way about her, too. If I thought someone wanted to hurt her now, I'd protect her no matter what it took. And not pushing her to tell me before she's ready? Well, that's the only way I can protect her today. Until she brings it up, I will love her and wait till she's ready.

Whenever that is, I'll be waiting.

12.9 Nashville, 2015

Probity

It just doesn't seem right that someone can do something bad to someone else, but it's the person it was done *to* who has to pay for it the rest of their whole lives. Anyway, being turned down by VOCA got me thinking about how I might not be able to get the money from them to pay for my therapy, but I sure would've liked to have had justice. I knew I never would, since by then all my perpetrators were dead. I'd never even get the satisfaction of a confession, or even an apology. But I *really* would've liked to. And *that* got me thinking about all the other victims, too, whose perpetrators weren't dead yet.

So, I went down to the Tennessee State Library and Archives and got the legislative history guy whose name was Vince to help me look up the laws about prosecuting child abuse so I could see exactly what they said. Maybe I could do something that would help make it better for those who came after me, you know? After I told him what I needed and while he was looking it all up, I was walking around, looking at stuff they had for people to look at. Pictures hanging on the walls. Pamphlets. Stuff like that.

One of them was a pamphlet that had a bunch of pictures in it of people in my state who'd been elected over the years. I was thumbing through it, just passing time while I was waiting, when all of a sudden I couldn't breathe. I doubled over and it felt like I was being crushed under an elephant. One of the pictures was of someone I knew. I'd seen him before, in the dark, around a fire. One of the guys in the pictures was one of the bad guys. And when I saw his name, I knew just who he was. He was from Bumblebee.

When I got back from throwing up I paid for the copies of all the stuff Vince had found, and sat down to read through everything he'd so kindly printed off for me. When I did, I came across something else that shook me through and through.

Right there, on a paper telling about the history of a Tennessee law that created a "one year after the eighteenth birthday" statute of limitations deadline for pressing child abuse charges against a perpetrator, it gave the names of all the men who were instrumental in the passing of the law, and one of their leaders was the man I'd just recognized.

And in that moment, I knew just how it was that they could get away with it all that time. It wasn't enough that they had a sheriff's deputy involved, and a mortician, too, to protect the guilty and help dispose of the bodies. It wasn't enough that they had the resources of an entire federal agency behind them to research the most effective way to hurt somebody. They'd even made sure one of them got elected to the state legislature and the very first year he was in office, he'd engineered and finessed through the process a bill that would have kept any of them from ever facing child abuse charges in the future, no matter how far down the line. Even supposing that any of us lived long enough to leave home, and remembered what they'd done, and somehow overcame our fear of reporting them, they'd still get off scot-free. They had all the bases covered. Every single one.

12.10 NASHVILLE, 1987

Doc

You may never know how much was staged and how much was not. But in either event, the end result is the same: for you, it really happened.

It wasn't your fault.

They could be anywhere, but they are not everywhere.

If they were in the majority, they wouldn't need to convince their victims to keep their actions secret.

It's okay if you think about it.

It's okay if you don't think about it.

It may *feel* real, but it isn't happening now.

You have already lived through it. Now all you have to do is live through remembering it.

There will always be some people who would stop it if they knew.

They can never make you go back to not knowing you can ask for help.

You are safe now; your children are safe now; you can protect yourself and your children.

There are more good people in the world than there are bad people.

In the short run evil may be more powerful than good, but good is more persistent.

You don't have to do it—no matter what it is— today.

12.11 NASHVILLE, 2015

PROBITY

It's taken decades of therapy and fighting to stay alive day after day to get to where I'm not so depressed and torn up inside every minute. I'm not quite so angry at myself anymore, or as distrusting of everybody else, whether they'd had anything to do with all the stuff that happened to me or not.

Once I figured out what my memories were pointing to, I started looking stuff up, and I discovered lots of other people about my age have remembered things like I have, too, and that there are folks all over the United States and Canada who've reported the same sorts of things to their own doctors. I even met a few other survivors, one of whom, without knowing I was from there, told me bad things had happened to her in Bumblebee. We remembered lots of the same things, but we didn't remember each other. Most folks said the idea for hurting us had been traced all the way back to the CIA. That made me even more afraid.

Then, not long ago, I was mugged and was invited to talk about it at a VOCA speak-out, where victims stand up and tell their stories in front of news cameras and a bunch of people they don't know. I said I would, but sometimes things don't work out the way you planned.

The person making out the program called the place I worked to ask me what my topic was, but on the day they called I was out of the office. When I wasn't there, the caller asked if anyone else knew what my topic was, and one of the few people who knew I was a survivor of this stuff mistakenly told them she guessed that's what it was, instead. Before I knew it—and without my knowledge or consent—there I was in the printed and publicized program, right between victim of vehicular assault and survivor of homicide attempt: Probity Jones, survivor of satanic ritual abuse.

When you're constantly afraid the bad guys will kill you or someone you love if they find you, that's not exactly the sort of thing you want people to know. As soon as I discovered I'd been outed without my permission, I found myself once again doubled over in terror, not able to breathe, and puking my guts out in the closest bathroom. After I calmed down enough and had a chance to think about it, though, I realized maybe I had a responsibility to tell my story because by then all of my perpetrators were dead. No other survivor I'd met by then could say that. Just me.

So, I went around and asked every other survivor I knew at the time what they'd want people to know, if they had a chance to speak out. And every one of them, every single one, said what they'd want people to know is that it really happens. So when I stood up there on that stage that night, that's what I said. And then I said this:

"Our abusers were able to control what our bodies did; where we went; what we ate, heard, and saw. They could take advantage of our innocence, our trust, and our faith. They could leave us wounded, abused, and afraid. But they couldn't take away who we were to the core."

I paused to steady myself as the room filled with thunderous applause. The sudden outpouring of support was a resounding affirmation of every single victim of every kind of abuse—a wordless reminder that whether or not we survived, our lives matter. *We* matter.

All victims suffer. We all endure. But we are not reduced to that. We are *not* what they did to us. We will *always* be that kernel of who we are that the abusers could not touch.

The crowd that night cheered for all of us: Those who lived. Those who died. Those who remember every detail, and those whose memories are impaired. Those whose scars are visible, and those whose wounds cannot be seen.

And if you are a survivor, too, they were cheering for *you*.

When the room was quiet once again, I ended with these words: "I can't speak for anybody else, but I can speak for myself. In my case, the only variable in the entire equation they couldn't control was me."

EPILOGUE

"I was dreaming about your father," Little Boy said when he awoke. "He said to tell you he was sorry. He said to tell you that he thought what he did was for the best, but he was wrong."

I glanced at the boy in the rearview mirror; he had been sleeping in the backseat. I wasn't sure how to react.

"Your grandparents were there, too," he went on as he rubbed the sleep out of his eyes, hugged me around the headrest, and kissed me on the cheek. "But they didn't say they were sorry about anything. Only your father said that. Your grandmother said she taught you how to cook and to sew, and your grandfather said he taught you to garden and to love the earth. Your father didn't say what he did, but he said now he knew he was wrong, and to tell you he was sorry."

I was astounded. The boy was just five years old at the time and had never met any of the people he had just mentioned. In fact, I had rarely even spoken of them. Well, at least, he had never met them in the usual sense.

They had all died within the span of just a few years, a period which ended five years before his birth.

That particular day was my father's death day, the day on which I traditionally made my annual pilgrimage to my hometown and the cemetery where all three of them were buried. My very own personal Memorial Day.

On that day, as I had done a dozen times before, I had driven the two hours each way to visit the cemetery which houses our family plot, to talk to those who had gone before. Not only are my father and grandparents buried there, but also an uncle who had died when he was just a boy, and a few others I never knew.

L.B. had ridden with me that year for the first and only time, wandering among the tombstones and contentedly throwing himself into piles of brightly colored leaves while I talked to the dead. He eventually came over to join me, bright blue eyes sparkling.

"What's the matter?" he asked.

"Oh, I'm just sad," I replied. I wasn't sure just how much to explain. "I'm sad they never got to meet you. They'd have really liked you," I went on, "and I think you would have liked them."

"Introduce me," he demanded. "I want to meet them."

And so, bemused, I did so. As though they could hear, I went through a formal introduction, introducing the child who is my legacy to the ancestors who were my past. "Son, this is your great-grandmother Willie and your great-grandfather Hunter. And over there is my father, your grandfather. Gent died when I was twelve years old. Granddad died not long after, and

Grandma died one night during a lightning storm while I was out on a date with your dad."

I hadn't the slightest idea how to continue. Addressing the tombstones, I went on. "And this is my son, your grandson and great-grandson. L.B. is smart and happy and funny and strong, and he loves to play soccer. You can't see him, but he has the same blond hair I had when I was his age, beautiful blue eyes, and a tan that puts to shame every sunburn I have ever had. I love him very much." I paused. "I think you would, too."

"Thank you," he somberly replied, and then he wandered off again. Later, we both climbed back into the car to start the long drive home. For a while, he slept in the backseat while I drove. It was when he awoke that he told me of his strange dream. "I was dreaming about your father. He said to tell you he was sorry..." It was not the first time my child had a dream I couldn't explain. It wouldn't be the last.

I need to remember this, even if it is only a dream, I thought. *So much of my life has been forgotten, but this day, this moment, this dream of L.B.'s is something I want never to forget. This*—this—*is worth writing down. It is probably the only apology I will ever get.*

Remember this, I said to myself, *remember.*

Like my Grandmomma and Granddaddy used to say,

Don't fret, Little Bit. It's all gonna be okay.
Remember what Lao Tzu said:

"What a caterpillar calls THE END of the world,
the world calls a butterfly."

*"...until the lions have their own historians,
the history of the hunt will always glorify the hunter...*

*Once I realized that, I had to be a writer.
I had to be that historian.
It's not one man's job. It's not one person's job.
But it is something we have to do,
so that the story of the hunt will also reflect the agony,
the travail—the bravery, even, of the lions."*

CHINUA ACHEBE, Quoted in *THE PARIS REVIEW, Winter 1994*

Afterword

In the aftermath of Watergate, and at the direction of then-Director of the CIA Richard Helms, the majority of the records pertaining to MKUltra were destroyed in 1973. In spite of that action, four years later Freedom of Information Act requests were able to "follow the money" to approximately fifteen thousand declassified financial documents which had accidentally escaped destruction. These records documented that at least eighty institutions—including pharmaceutical companies, research foundations, institutions of higher education, hospitals, and clinics—along with approximately one hundred eighty-five researchers in both the United States and Canada, many of whom did not know where the funding for their research originated, were inadvertently providing their results to the CIA.

Funded projects included, but were not limited to, research into torture; drugs; physical, sexual, and emotional abuse; sleep deprivation; electronic stimulation; isolation; and hypnotism. Many of the projects involved experimenting on military personnel and civilians, both children and adults, without their knowledge or consent. Current U.S. policies regarding the necessity of informed consent from research subjects were developed as a direct result of the discovery of these post-Nuremberg human rights violations, which occurred on North American soil.

One of MKUltra's projects—the one called "Monarch," along with its many subprojects—focused its research on ways the United States could more successfully interrogate other nationals, while at the same time insulating its own human resources from the interrogations of others. In theory, one objective of Project Monarch was to subject a volunteer trainee to the experiences necessary for a separate spy personality to form, one that could be accessed only by a certain combination of words or events. Only the handler or handlers would have the key. This idea (minus the willing volunteer) was fictionalized in 1959 into the book and later movie *The Manchurian Candidate*, in which one prisoner of war was brainwashed into becoming an assassin, while others were brainwashed into believing he was a hero.

Memories of the actual events behind that fiction vary.

ACKNOWLEDGMENTS

My real parents, aunts, uncles, cousins, siblings, and children. Lest anyone ask you if this really happened, please refer them to these words on the copyright page: *This is a work of fiction.* In reality, each of you surpasses anything to which my words have the ability to do justice. My life is enriched by loving you all.

Kathie, I thank you from the bottom of my heart for your pertinacious believing in and telling of your truth, even when others did not wish to hear it. In fact, especially then.

Two Hearts in Love, the best cheerleaders in the world. Readers Theater! Oh, my goodness! Who knew you'd hold the key?

My very own Little Boy, now the delightful and compassionate husband of a beautiful and brilliant wife, father of his own Little Boy with a Little Girl on the way. You once had the dream that started this quest; thank you for sharing it with me.

My favorite shrink. You know who you are. Without you, this book would never have been written and my entire life would have been greatly diminished. Thank you for helping me put words and order to the cacophony in my mind, and especially for every day you've helped me stay alive, for the most part, two weeks at a time.

My last child left living at home. Thank you so much for being so patient. I'm almost done with this part. Could you just give me five more minutes?

My best friends in all the world, Deborah and Terri, plus the many who have befriended me during the course of my life, including (but not limited to) Arthur; Beverly; Charles; Doug and Mickey; Earline; Glenda; Harmon; Ingrid; Janet and Bill; Jay; Jim and Tony; Joyce; Judy; Mac; Mark; Martha; Mary; Mauni; Moses; Nancy; Nita; Pat; Quio; Sandy; Susan; and oh, thank you, thank you, thank you very much, Bonnie. I would never have made it without each and every one of you. You are absolutely the best. No, *you* are. No, seriously. YOU are.

The magnificent Angela, George, Ginger, Robert, Sally, and Tracy, editors and proofreaders extraordinaire. I simply can't say enough about you. And I'm sure you would all agree that in every other regard I tend to say way too much.

The amazing Susan, translator of all my favorite phrases. You are indeed the epitome of all things bookish. I want to be you when I grow up.

Paula, you cut right through to the heart of things. You immediately and astutely discerned that few readers would get what the chrysalis was if I didn't put a butterfly on the back cover with it. Okay! You were right! I was wrong!

Bill, I greatly appreciate the hours you spent talking with me about growing up gay and closeted in the era of Gent's youth. It made all the difference in the world. Thank you.

Vince in Legislative History at the Tennessee State Library and Archives, this book wouldn't have been the same without you. I am so grateful you found that stuff! Thank you for all of your help.

My GoFundMe sponsors, in order of appearance: Candace Thompson, Barb and Terry Gould, Gary and Terri Johnson, Dixie and Doug Steidinger, Ginger Manley, Melanie Blievernicht, Betsy Thorpe, Sally Rodes Lee, Jeff Thompson, Sandy Madsen, Barry Sulkin, and You-Who-Wish-Not-To-Be-Named. Thank you, each and every one, for making this possible... before the year 2045, when I'd be ninety.

Many of the people listed above either read or listened to large portions of this book as it was being written. To each of you, for all your feedback, thank you. You deserve all the credit for the good parts. The failures are unreservedly mine.

To the folks who have let me know over the years that parts and pieces of this story ring true for them, thank you more than words can adequately say. One of you, years ago, said to me out of the blue, "My grandparents used to take me over six hundred miles each way to Bumblebee, Tennessee, for the rituals." Another let me know her mentor at a children's psychiatric hospital had told her late one night that all those years he'd been traveling back and forth to

Washington he'd been conducting experiments on human subjects and consulting secretly for the CIA. Two more held pieces they had no way of knowing I needed in order to make the entire scenario make sense, and without their knowing I needed them, shared them in such a way that they made it round to me.

To Colin Ross, M.D., writer of the original Freedom of Information Act request which revealed the first fifteen thousand (more or less) financial records documenting MKUltra's involvement in mind control experiments, I am deeply grateful. Thank you for all you have done on behalf of survivors everywhere.

And to you, Dear Reader, thank you for buying and reading my book. To call this particular work "historical fiction" somehow doesn't quite get it. "Fictionalized history" might be more precise. There have been reports from clinicians, researchers, and survivors all across the United States and Canada that the CIA actually did fund programs such as Chrysalis. A single victim of such abuse would have been too many. The truth is worse: they number too many to count. Some died when they wanted to live; others lived out the rest of their lives wishing they had been the ones who died instead. Please help me keep their memories alive, so that neither their suffering nor their deaths will have been in vain.

M.C. Nelson
January 1, 2015

❖ PASSAGES MARKED BY BULLETED WARNINGS:

6.6   Marion, a prostitute, describes being attacked by Gent.

7.3   Employees of The Company discuss how to keep the children from talking.

7.4   Gent discusses the protocol for human sacrifices.

7.8   Probity talks about her family's rituals on the nights of group meetings.

8.1   Company employees discuss the protocol they are developing.

8.7   Company employees continue their discussion of the protocol.

9.5   One of the Bumblebee group members incites the group to murder a human adult.

9.7   Probity describes Gent's abduction of an adult.

9.8   Charlie confronts Gent about losing control of himself and the group.

10.2   Leo describes his fear that more subjects may be killed at the Bumblebee site.

10.3   Martin describes his reluctance to report Gent's murder of one of the Bumblebee subjects to his superiors.

10.4 Gent elaborates on his desire to sacrifice Armleuchter at the next meeting.

10.8 Gent considers his impending death at the hands of the group.

11.3 Armleuchter describes his plan for revenge.

11.4 Probity talks about her mother's upcoming marriage to Armleuchter.

11.10 Mama describes the method she used to convince Leo to let her be the one to kill Gent during the group's Halloween ritual.

12.6 Deed tells his side of what happened the day he died.

❖ PASSAGES MARKED BY FULL PAGE WARNINGS:

7.9   Gent describes some of the techniques used to force the children to watch the rituals.

8.2   Gent describes the protocol used to keep the children from telling anyone else what is going on.

8.5   Armleuchter describes looking forward to hurting the children.

8.6.   Probity describes her feelings during a night around the fire.

8.8   Gent describes an effort to get Probity to splinter into multiple personalities.

9.6   Gent describes sacrificing a human adult.

9.10   Probity describes Gent murdering one of the children.

10.7   Mama describes what she sees one night when she follows Gent and Probity to the site of the rituals.

12.5   Probity describes some of the images that haunt her. Extreme, graphic imagery.

CPSIA information can be obtained
at www.ICGtesting.com
Printed in the USA
LVHW112008280921
698769LV00005B/47